The Old Gatehouse

S Stanley Scott.

The Old Gatehouse

STANLEY SCOTT

ISBN: 978-1-78324-213-9

Published by Wordzworth
www.wordzworth.com

To my family
With love

CHAPTER 1

Caiston Manor was a large Country House built in the early seventeenth century. It stood in ten thousand acres of farm and woodland in the Hertfordshire countryside. The Manor was surrounded by lawns and gardens, with a tree-lined drive leading down to the Old Gatehouse, which was in a poor state of repair, having been shut up for many years. The last family who lived there had lost their little girl in a drowning accident in the lake at the end of the garden. The memory of this tragedy still lingered on in some people's minds.

The present owner of the Manor was Lord Barnes, a wealthy banker, who had recently returned from abroad, where he had been exploring the caves and tombs of Ancient Egypt, together with Charles Rupert, another wealthy businessman.

It was thought that Lord Barnes was not married, but there was rumour that he had had an affair with a married woman while out in Egypt. Felix, Lord Barnes' manservant, a man of few words, would not throw any light on his master's love life, only to say there had been times when Lord Barnes had been seen in female company.

Lord Barnes was in his study one morning when he heard someone knocking on the study door.

'Come in,' said Lord Barnes.

The door opened and Mrs Brookes, the housekeeper, announced, 'Mr Fanshaw is here to see you, my lord.'

'Show him in, Mrs Brookes.'

'Good morning, sir!'

'Good morning, George!' replied his lordship. 'What can I do for you?'

'I understand you are wanting help in recording and sorting out the items you brought home from abroad,' said the Head Gardener. 'My daughter, Lucy, is nearly eighteen years old now and is looking for something to do, and wondered if your lordship could do with some assistance?'

'I certainly could,' said Lord Barnes. 'Tell her to come and see me'.

'Thank you, sir,' said the Head Gardener, 'I'll do that.'

'How are things in the gardens after yesterday's rain?' enquired Lord Barnes.

'Looking much better this morning, my lord, I'm pleased to say.'

'It's nice to see you, George, thank you for looking in. I must not detain you any longer though!' said Lord Barnes.

'Good day, my lord.'

Making his way down to the kitchen, he met Mrs Brookes who enquired, 'Is his lordship alone now, Mr Fanshaw?'

'Yes, Mrs Brookes - he was a few minutes ago. I thought I might beg a cup of tea before returning to the gardens!'

'You will find them all having their mid-morning break,' said Mrs Brookes, 'you've timed it just right!'

Caiston Manor had six bedrooms reserved for guests, and a number of other rooms for those staff who lived-in. Nearby, were cottages occupied by workers of the estate including the Head Gardener, his wife and his daughter, Lucy, a kind and attractive young lady, always on the lookout for romance should the right young man come along. So, on the following Monday morning, she set off to see Lord Barnes.

When she arrived at the Manor she was met by Mrs Brookes, a friendly soul, but still in full charge of her position.

'My name is Lucy Fanshaw. I have come to see Lord Barnes,' said Lucy.

'Come with me,' said Mrs Brookes, and took Lucy to the study.

Lord Barnes was pleased to see Lucy, and told her about his travels abroad. Then he took her to the room where some of the things he had brought back were stored.

'How soon could you start, Lucy?'

'Well, er, -on Wednesday, my Lord,' said Lucy, being taken aback at his lordship's eagerness to get started.

'You can use the room where we have just been as your place of work,' said Lord Barnes. 'That is your room from now on.'

When Lucy arrived home, her mother wanted to know how she had got on.

'Very well!' said Lucy. 'I think his lordship likes me. He has given me a room to work in all to myself, and Mrs Brookes was kind to me when I arrived. I think I shall like working there.'

'His lordship has always been good to your father,' said Lucy's mother, 'so I am sure you will be alright.'

The day arrived for Lucy to start work. When she arrived at the Manor she was met by Mrs Brookes.

'His lordship is busy at the moment, so I'll take you to your room.'

After a short while, Mrs Brookes reappeared at the door and said, 'Lucy, his lordship is going to be occupied for a while longer, so I will take you down to the kitchen to meet Mrs Plum, the cook, and Freda.'

When they entered the kitchen, they found Freda Sharp, the scullery maid, washing up at the sink.

'Hello,' said Lucy.

Freda Sharp looked up.

'Hello,' said Freda.

Lucy recognized her at once as being seen with some of the boys in the village. Lucy also noticed Freda had a dirty apron on.

Mrs Brookes said to Lucy, 'Most of his lordship's treasures are in the room where you will be working, but the very special items are locked away in a room upstairs. His lordship said you would be coming this morning to start work, and if he was busy when you arrived, I was to show you around the rooms downstairs.'

Lucy's room was at the rear of the Manor. It had a large window looking out over the back lawn. The room had a high ceiling, and a fireplace on one wall nearby the desk where Lucy would be working. It was so full there wasn't much space to move around in. 'Still,' thought Lucy, 'I'm sure I shall be happy here.'

Not long after Lucy had arrived, Lord Barnes reappeared.

'Has Mrs Brookes been looking after you?' he enquired, with a smile.

'Yes, your lordship,' said Lucy.

'I had to see the Farm Manager. You will soon find your way around and Mrs Brookes will always help if you want to know anything when I'm not here.'

After several days had passed, it was clear that Lord Barnes was enjoying having Lucy around, and as for Lucy, she was happy to be doing something useful. However, she had noticed a certain amount of disapproval from Felix, Lord Barnes' man-servant, but as she rarely came in contact with him, it didn't bother her much. On the other hand, Mrs Brookes was fond of Lucy, and said she was like a breath of fresh air.

One morning, a few days later, as Lucy was returning to her room after having a cup of tea with Mrs Brookes in the kitchen, she heard loud voices coming from the study. Suddenly the door flew open and a red-faced Felix came out, making his way to the door and into the garden, followed by a stream of angry words from his lordship. Lucy quickly shut the door of her room and got on with her work.

Next morning, when Lucy arrived, she was met by Mrs Brookes, who said that his lordship had gone away and she did not know when he would be back, but that he would send word when he was returning. Felix was nowhere to be seen, but it was thought he had gone with his lordship.

Three days after this, a letter arrived for his lordship, bearing a foreign postmark. This, and several other letters, were taken to the study by Mrs Brookes, to await the return of his lordship.

Mrs Brookes and Lucy were having a cup of tea that afternoon in the kitchen, when they saw Nigel Blair, the Farm Manager, coming across the lawn towards the kitchen door.

'Have you heard when his lordship is returning?' enquired Nigel Blair.

'No!' replied Mrs Brookes. 'This is not like his lordship. He has always been so particular about keeping in touch.'

'We were just having a cup of tea, would you like one?' asked Mrs Plum.

'I'm afraid I can't stop,' said Nigel, '-you see, I have a horse that is not well, and since his lordship is not here, I best get back to the farm to deal with it myself. I think I'd better call in the vet.'

CHAPTER 2

Next day, when Lucy was having her morning cup of tea with Mrs Brookes and Freda Sharp, they heard the front door bell ring.

'I wonder who that can be?' said Mrs Brookes.

'If it is his lordship,' said Lucy, 'he'd best not see me here'.

'I'd better go and see who it is,' said Mrs Brookes. When she opened the door she saw a tall young man standing there holding a suitcase.

'Good morning, ma'am,' said the man. 'My name is Percival Rupert. I did write to say I was coming. This is Lord Barnes' house?'

'Yes,' replied Mrs Brookes, 'but his lordship is away at the moment. Well, you had better come in'.

'Thank you. My father was with Lord Barnes in Egypt and I have travelled a long way to discuss the artefacts he brought back with him. As I said, I wrote to him when I was abroad.'

Mrs Brookes remembered the envelope with the foreign stamp and showed it to the young man.

'Yes, that's it,' he said, '-that's my writing.'

'Well,' said Mrs Brookes, 'I'm not sure when his lordship will be back, but if you'd care to stay here tonight, we can sort something out tomorrow if there is still no news of his return. If you bring your case, I will show you to a room.'

As Mrs Brookes and the young man climbed the stairs, the young man caught sight of Lucy returning to her room.

'Who is that?' asked the young man.

'Oh, that is a member of staff,' replied Mrs Brookes.

After she had shown Percival Rupert to his room, Mrs Brookes went back downstairs to find Lucy.

'I should keep your door shut from now on,' she said, 'because I don't like the look of him -he's got shifty eyes, so be on your guard.'

As Mrs Brookes was leaving Lucy's room, she saw the young man coming down the stairs.

'I think I will pay a visit to the village. I will be back later on this evening,' said the young man. At that he went out of the front door.

It was quite a walk from the Manor down the drive to the village, but as he passed the Old Gatehouse, he stopped and looked at the old building, as though he had seen it before but could not remember where.

Later on that evening, the young man returned to the Manor somewhat the worse for drink. He made his way up the stairs to his room and flopped down on the bed. This is how he was found the next morning by the maid when she brought him an early cup of tea, -still fully clothed, fast asleep and snoring loudly.

Mrs Brookes was in the dining room putting the final touches to the breakfast table when the young man appeared at the door.

'Good morning!' he said.

'Good morning!' replied Mrs Brookes.

'You must forgive me if I seem rather distant, I had quite an evening of it at your local inn. I hope I haven't disgraced myself'.

'No, you haven't,' replied Mrs Brookes.

'Have you any news of Lord Barnes' return?' enquired the young man.

'No, I have no idea' said Mrs Brookes.

'-Only I must see Lord Barnes about some of the artefacts belonging to my father, -who by the way is ill in hospital. There is some dispute over ownership.'

'I'm sure his lordship wouldn't do anything wrong,' said Mrs Brookes. 'He certainly wouldn't take anything that wasn't his, there must be some mistake.'

'I don't think so,' replied the young man. 'Before I left to come here, my father told me what happened out in Egypt -a very sordid story I can tell you, but I won't bore you with the details.'

Mrs Brookes was worried on hearing this and hurried off to the kitchen to recover from what she had just heard.

After breakfast, the young man decided to take a walk around the grounds and Mrs Brookes relayed to Lucy some of what she had just been told.

'I hope there isn't going to be trouble,' said Mrs Brookes. 'This man means business.'

'Well I hope he doesn't come bothering me!' said Lucy.

During the afternoon Mrs Brookes answered the front door to a tall man dressed in a dark suit, wearing a trilby-style hat.

'Good afternoon, ma'am. I'm lnspector Jakes. Could I see you for a moment please?'

'Yes,' replied Mrs Brookes, 'come in. I am Housekeeper here at Caiston Manor.' She showed him into the study.

'I am making inquiries about Lord Barnes,' said the Inspector.

'I'm very sorry, sir,' said Mrs Brookes, 'but his lordship is away and we don't know when he will be home.'

'I don't think he will be home just yet,' said the Inspector. 'He has been arrested for attempted murder'.

'Oh no!' gasped Mrs Brookes.

'You had better sit down,' said the Inspector, seeing Mrs Brookes was upset.

'I can't believe it!' said Mrs Brookes.

'I'm afraid it's true,' said the Inspector.

After Mrs Brookes had recovered from the shock of the news she had just received, the Inspector asked her for the names of any persons visiting the Manor.

'Well, we have one person staying here at the moment -a man called Percival Rupert. The rest are staff.'

'Where is this man now?' enquired the Inspector.

'He went out for a walk in the grounds.'

'I must speak to him straight away, and then I will return to have a word with you before I leave. Please excuse me for the moment,' said the Inspector. 'Now I must find Mr Percival Rupert!'

At that, Mrs Brookes showed the Inspector out.

Lucy was in her room, working, when she was aware she was being watched. On looking up at the window, she was horrified to see Mr Rupert trying to attract her attention, but then the Inspector appeared and took him away. She heaved a sigh of relief and made her way to the kitchen, where she found Mrs Brookes giving Cook instructions for the evening meal.

'I think that man wanted to get into my room!' exclaimed Lucy.

'Where is he now?' asked Mrs Brookes.

'I think he is with the Inspector at the moment. I best

get back to my room though, I don't want him in there,' said Lucy.

As she entered the hall with Mrs Brookes, who had accompanied her to make sure she got back safely, there was someone banging on the front door.

'Gracious me!' exclaimed Mrs Brookes. 'Whoever can that be?'

On opening the door, there stood the young man together with the Inspector. 'Can we come in?' asked the Inspector.

Mrs Brookes stood to one side to let them enter.

'May we use the study?' asked the Inspector.

'You may,' replied Mrs Brookes.

From then on, all was quiet, and shortly afterwards the Inspector left. As for the young man, he returned to his room and didn't want to discuss his encounter with the police, only to say he hoped it would be fruitful.

CHAPTER 3

The following day, the Estates Manager asked Mrs Brookes to assemble her staff in the hall as he had some news to report. He would be at the Manor mid-morning, after he had visited the Farm Manager and Estate workers.

'I wonder what he is going to tell us?' asked Lucy.

'Perhaps we are all going to get the sack!' exclaimed Freda Sharp.

'I hope not,' said Edith Plum. 'I haven't finished paying for that dress I sent away for. My husband is always going on at me for buying things from a catalogue.'

When the Estates Manager arrived, he said what he had to tell them must be kept to themselves, and not talked about in the village.

'It appears,' said Mr Parry, 'that his lordship had been accused of strangling someone,'

'What?' interrupted Mrs Brookes, 'His lordship would never do anything like that. I know him too well, he wouldn't hurt a fly!'

'Don't be too alarmed, Mrs Brookes, it has now been proved that he was nowhere near the scene of the crime at the time. It has also come to light that his lordship was once married and has a son of twenty. It is thought that his lordship's wife died whilst he was away in Egypt, and his son was entrusted to the care of his aunt. What I have just told you has not yet been confirmed, and when I learn the true facts I will let you all know. I understand his lordship will be bringing his son with him when he returns.'

'Do we know when this is likely to be?' enquired Mrs Brookes.

'Not at the moment. I understand there are a few details to be sorted out first, concerning ownership of some of the things his lordship brought back from abroad,' replied Mr Parry.

'-And what has happened to his lordship's man-servant?' asked Mrs Brookes.

'He's not been heard of since the day he left,' said Mr Parry. 'That's all I have to say at the moment.'

'Thank you for putting us in the picture, Mr Parry. We must all go about our business now, but before you go, I have a matter of some urgency which I should like to discuss with you. Perhaps, if you can spare a moment, you would follow me to the study?'

'Certainly,' replied Mr Parry, following Mrs Brookes across the hall. 'There's just one thing the police have left to clear up: they still don't know who the attacker was. Apparently it's not the first time the victim has been attacked.'

'Well I hope the police soon catch him,' said Mrs Brookes.

'Now, perhaps you will tell me what is bothering you?' said Mr Parry.

'Last night,' replied Mrs Brookes, 'when I was going to bed, I happened to look out of the window at the end of the corridor leading to my room, and I'm sure I saw a light coming from the Old Gatehouse. It's not the first time I've seen a light there and it doesn't stay on for long. I thought I was seeing things at first, but when I saw it a second time I decided I had better say something to you.'

'I will look into it,' said Mr Parry. 'That place hasn't been lived in for years.'

'I shall be glad when his lordship is back,' said Mrs Brookes, 'I've a number of things to discuss with him.'

'So have I,' replied Mr Parry. 'The list seems to get longer every day!'

'By the way,' said Mrs Brookes. 'I almost forgot, Lucy mentioned to me the other day that she can't open one of the windows in her room, it seems to be stuck.'

'I will get Mr Jolly to have a look at it,' replied Mr Parry. 'Incidentally, Mrs Brookes, is that fellow still staying here?'

'Yes,' said Mrs Brookes with a frown. 'I don't like the man and I don't trust him. His lordship won't be very pleased to find him here when he returns. I shall be glad when he's gone!'

'Well, I must be on my way. I'll send Mr Jolly round to see to Lucy's window. Good-bye.'

Several days later, a letter arrived from his lordship, asking for Mr Parry to collect him from the station, and stating he would be bringing his son home with him. Mrs Brookes was beside herself when she heard the news.

'I will get everything ready for them. His son can have that room looking out over the Park. It gets the sun first thing in the morning -he will love being there!'

'I wonder what he will be like?' said Lucy when she heard the news.

'I bet he's a spoiled brat!' said Freda Sharp. 'Those type usually are.'

'Well, we shall have to make him welcome whatever he's like,' said Lucy, '-he's his lordship's son.'

The news soon spread around the village.

'I hope his lordship doesn't bring that Felix back with him!' said Mrs Brookes. 'I never could get on with him.

If you ask me, he's a bad lot!'

'I didn't like him either,' said Lucy.

'By the way, Lucy, I told Mr Parry about your window and he is going to get Mr Jolly round to fix it.'

'Who's Mr Jolly?' said Lucy, trying hard not to laugh.

'He's the Estate's carpenter. He's a friendly man and lives up to his name!' said Mrs Brookes, with a grin on her face. 'He lives in one of the cottages over on the far side of the Estate.'

At last the day came when Lord Barnes and his son arrived home. Mr Parry had been to collect them both from the station, and had arranged a special home-coming for them. Staff and workers from the Estate lined the steps leading up to the front door, and a loud cheer went up as father and son stepped out of the carriage. When the cheering subsided, his lordship thanked them for their welcome and announced proudly, 'This is my son, Michael, who will be living here with me at the Manor.'

Lord Barnes and Michael then went into the hall, followed by Mrs Brookes.

'We have a visitor staying here who is wanting to see you, my lord,' said Mrs Brookes.

'What's his name?' enquired Lord Barnes.

'Mr Percival Rupert, sir'.

'What's that man doing in my house? Tell him to pack his bags and go -I don't want to see him!'

With that, Lord Barnes turned and went into his study,

muttering something under his breath. Mrs Brookes said to Michael, 'Come with me and I will show you to your room.'

She took Michael across the hall and up the stairs. On the way, they saw Lucy returning to her room.

'Who's that?' enquired Michael.

'That's Lucy. She works here, helping your father to record the things he brought back from abroad. Her father works on the Estate. He's the head gardener here. We also have Freda who works in the kitchen helping Mrs Plum, the cook. Then there's Florence and Maud -the two housemaids,' went on Mrs Brookes, with a twinkle in the eye.

'I think I'm going to like it here!' smiled Michael.

'I hope so,' replied Mrs Brookes. 'I expect his lordship will want to show you round the Estate when you've settled in. Can you ride a horse?'

'I have never tried!' said Michael.

'Well, I'm sure you will soon learn. You will certainly need a horse to get about the Estate. I must go and see his lordship now, as I've a number of things to discuss with him. If there's anything else you want to know, you will find me in my room downstairs,' said Mrs Brookes, opening the door to Michael's room.

All sorts of stories were being bandied about the village concerning Lord Barnes. Who was the young man he had brought back with him? -and if it was his son, where was Lord Barnes' wife? -and what were the police doing asking questions at the Manor in Lord Barnes' absence?

Little did they know there was even more intrigue unfolding right under their noses.

CHAPTER 4

The next day, Mr Parry went to see Mrs Brookes. He had some news to tell her.

'Do you remember you asked me to find out about the light you saw at the Old Gatehouse?' enquired Mr Parry. 'Well, I had a good look round the place, but didn't see anything wrong -only a few cobwebs and dust, though it did look as if someone had been walking back and forth on the path leading from the back of the house down to the jetty. The garden is like a wilderness. It was always well-cared for -it's a shame to see it so neglected. I couldn't see any signs of a break in, but I will keep a lookout in the hope of finding out what is going on there.'

'Thank you, Mr Parry,' said Mrs Brookes, 'I will let you know if I see any more lights.'

Meantime, Michael was beginning to find his way around the downstairs rooms. He discovered mid-morning was a good time to visit the kitchen, as most of the staff were having their morning cup of tea. It also gave him the chance to talk to Lucy, using the excuse he was interested in the work she was doing. This didn't go down very well with Freda, the scullery maid, or the two house-maids, because Michael wasn't showing any interest in them. Mrs Brookes was soon aware of what was happening, and suggested that Michael should go riding each morning with his lordship in order to get used to finding his way around the Estate on his own. This would perhaps help ward off any trouble between members of her staff when they were having their morning break!

Michael soon learned to ride, and was often seen out with his lordship, but he always tried to see Lucy every chance he got. One day, while out riding with his lordship, they called on the Farm Manager who had had an accident on the farm, injuring his right arm. When they knocked on the door, it was opened by an attractive young woman who asked them inside.

Lord Barnes enquired as to how Mr Blair was.

'Father is doing nicely, he will be so pleased to see you, my lord. -Father, look who has come to see you!'

'How is your arm progressing, Nigel? I hope you are not in too much pain."

'I'm getting on nicely thank you, your lordship,' said the Farm Manager. 'Phillis and her mother have been looking after me very well. -I don't think you have met my daughter, Phillis before. She has just finished at boarding school, and is looking for a post as a governess. There is certainly no chance of me stepping out of line with two of them keeping an eye on me!' he chuckled.

Although Michael was interested in Lucy, here was another young lady he rather liked the look of, and it was clear from the glances he was getting from her that she was interested in him too.

'Do you go riding very much?' Phillis asked Michael.

'Quite a lot. Since I have been home I go every day.'

'Have you seen the bluebells in Chaines Wood?'

'No,' replied Michael, 'I haven't.'

'Would you like to?' said Phillis. 'We could go this afternoon if you are free.'

'Alright!' said Michael, 'I will come here for you.'

Meanwhile, Lord Barnes had been chatting with his Farm Manager, and turning to Michael he said, 'Well my boy, we must be on our way.'

When the two of them left, Lord Barnes said to Michael, 'I know you are nearly twenty-one, but do be on your guard when you are with that young lady. I have heard a few stories concerning her reputation since she has been home, so just be careful when you are together!'

Arriving back at the Manor, Lord Barnes said to Michael, 'I must spend a little time with Lucy this afternoon. She said there was a problem with one of the crates. Some of it's contents are damaged.'

'If you would like me to help, I will come when I get back from my ride.'

After they had finished lunch, Lord Barnes went to Lucy's room to see the things which had been causing concern.

'If your lordship will look at these items, it seems as though they have been pulled about by someone not being careful. This statue has been broken and the arm is broken on this one too.'

Lord Barnes said, 'Did that Percival Rupert ever come in here?'

'Not while I was here,' said Lucy, 'but I can't say if he came in when I wasn't.'

'I will ask Mrs Brookes,' replied his lordship.

'Would you like me to go and fetch her?' asked Lucy.

'Yes, if you would.'

When Mrs Brookes came in, Lord Barnes asked her, 'Did you ever see Percival Rupert in this room, Mrs Brookes?'

'Well, yes. I caught sight of him coming out of the door one evening after Lucy had gone home.'

'Is he still around?' asked his lordship.

'No, thank goodness!' replied Mrs Brookes. 'He's gone.'

Turning to Lucy, Lord Barnes said, 'We had better check all the rest of the crates in case we find more broken items. Michael will be back later on this afternoon, so he will be able to help as well.'

It was nearly teatime before Michael arrived back. He didn't get a very good reception from his father when he entered the room.

'Where have you been?' asked Lord Barnes.

Looking a bit sheepish, Michael said, 'I'm sorry to be so late.'

'We could have done with your help earlier on, but thanks to Mrs Brookes, we have just finished. -By the way, Lucy, if you notice any discolouration on any of the objects while you are handling them, do let me know, as these things are used to being in very dry conditions.'

'Well, I have noticed a change on some items since I started here,' said Lucy.

'I was afraid of that,' said his lordship. 'I think we will have to have some form of heating installed in the place. Come Michael, I want to have a word with you,' said his lordship. 'We must leave Lucy to get on with her work.'

One morning, a few days later, when they were all in the kitchen having their morning break, Freda asked Lucy how she was getting on, adding 'I have heard we are to have some form of heating put in.'

'Yes!' said Mrs Brookes, butting in, 'his lordship will tell us about it all in good time.'

Lucy was surprised at Freda's interest in her work, in fact just recently, both of the housemaids as well as Freda had been more pleasant to her.

'My boyfriend,' said Freda, 'told me that he often sees Michael when he's out riding. Sometimes he goes riding with Phillis Blair, the Farm Manager's daughter. -In fact,' went on Freda, 'he's seen them out together most afternoons.'

'So that's where he's been!' thought Lucy. 'Now I know.'

'Time passes very quickly when you are busy,' said Mrs Brookes, one afternoon to his lordship.

'Yes it does,' said Lord Barnes. 'It will soon be my son's birthday. He will be twenty-one and I should like him to have a birthday party here, -one that he will remember. Perhaps you would give it some thought?'

'I will, sir,' replied Mrs Brookes.

'You might like to involve Lucy in your preparations,' said his lordship. 'She would be able to take some of the workload from your shoulders.'

'I think that would be a very good idea, sir'.

'I've grown to like her. She has worked very hard sorting and recording all my things.'

'She has always kept her place in the household,' said Mrs Brookes, 'and I'm very fond of her too.'

The next morning when Lucy arrived at work, Lord Barnes called her into the study.

'Now you have nearly finished in the downstairs room, and before we start on upstairs, I would like you to help Mrs Brookes get ready for my son's twenty-first birthday party. She will be glad of your help.'

'I should like that,' said Lucy. 'Is it to be held here at the Manor, my lord?'

'Yes, Lucy,' said his lordship, 'have a word with Mrs Brookes.'

It wasn't long before Lucy saw her, and together they worked out a plan of which they hoped his lordship would approve.

Two weeks before the party, Lucy was crossing the hall on her way to see Mrs Brookes, when she heard Michael's voice, 'Good morning Lucy!'

'Good morning Michael! Going riding again?'

'Only a short ride this morning, Lucy, -my father wants to see me about something. I hope it won't take long.'

When Lucy arrived at Mrs Brookes' room, she found her talking to Mr Parry.

'I saw that light again last night when I was going to my bed,' said Mrs Brookes. 'It's very strange, I can't make it out.'

'l will have another look today,' said Mr Parry. 'I've just got to have a word with his lordship then I'm off.'

It was nearly lunchtime when his lordship came in to see Mrs Brookes and Lucy.

'Have either of you seen Michael this morning?'

'Yes, my lord,' said Lucy. 'It was when I arrived this morning first thing. Michael said he was just going for a short ride to the woods, my lord.'

'Well, I wonder where he's got to? I had better find out what has happened. Meantime, if either of you should see him, please let me know.'

Suddenly there was banging on the front door, and when it was opened, there stood a worried Farm Manager.

'I must see his lordship immediately,' he said. 'Something has happened to Michael. He's been attacked!'

Hearing the commotion, Lord Barnes came out of his study.

'What has happened?'

'Michael was out riding when he was attacked by a man in the woods. One of the farm workers found him in a ditch. We have got him at our house and have sent for the doctor.'

'Take me to him at once!' demanded Lord Barnes.

'Come with me,' said the Farm Manager. 'I have my cart outside ready to take us there.'

About an hour later, his lordship arrived back at the Manor.

'Is Michael going to be alright, sir?' enquired Mrs Brookes.

'I think so,' said his lordship. 'He's been badly knocked about. Whoever did this will wish he had never been born! Michael is staying at the Blair's cottage tonight as he is too weak to move. The doctor said if all goes well he can be moved here tomorrow. Perhaps you would let the staff know what has happened, Mrs Brookes? I'm sure they must be worried.'

'They are, my lord.'

'The police are already asking questions in the village,' said Freda Sharp, when she arrived at work the next morning.

'You had best be getting on with the washing up, young lady!'

'Yes, Mrs Plum,' said Freda.

Just then, Mrs Brookes came into the kitchen.

'I've just shown the Police Inspector into the study to see his lordship. I think they might be there quite a while. Perhaps you would send in some refreshment for them presently?'

'I will get a tray ready,' said Mrs Plum.

About an hour later, a Police Sergeant arrived at the Manor to see the Inspector. He was shown into the study by Mrs Brookes.

'I have to report, sir,' said the sergeant, 'that an old lady in the village, while taking her dog for a walk, saw a man running down the road as if he was being chased. She thought he had come from the woods nearby, and what's more, she thought she had seen him before with his lordship.'

'Felix!' exclaimed Lord Barnes.

'Right!' said the Police Inspector. 'We must put out a call to detain this man. Will you put it in hand immediately, Sergeant?'

'Right away, sir!'

CHAPTER 5

It was late in the afternoon when they brought Michael back to the Manor. They carried him up to his room, accompanied by the doctor, who insisted Michael should spend a few days in bed to recover from his ordeal. The Inspector had said it would be wise if Michael stayed inside the Manor and did not go riding in the woods until the Police had apprehended his attacker. Lord Barnes sent for Mrs Brookes and asked her to make sure Michael had everything he needed. He thought it would be wise for staff to look in on Michael every now and then to make sure he was alright, and on no account was Michael to have any other visitors.

'I hope Michael will be well by the time his birthday comes,' said Mrs Brookes.

'Oh, I'm sure he will,' said his lordship, 'he's young, he'll soon mend.'

When Mrs Brookes returned to her room, she found Lucy waiting there.

'How is Michael? Is he going to be alright?'

'Yes, I think so,' said Mrs Brookes. 'A few days in bed will soon help him regain his strength.'

'What about his birthday party? -Will he be well enough to enjoy it?' enquired Lucy.

'His lordship has told me to carry on with the arrangements, although I think we have almost done as much as we can for the party. Most of the people who received invitations have replied, although we still haven't heard from the musicians, so I had better get in touch with them. Why don't you pay Michael a visit, Lucy? I'm sure he will be pleased to see you.'

Lucy didn't need telling twice. She thanked Mrs Brookes and made her way up to Michael's room. Tapping on the door, she heard a faint voice saying, 'come in.'

Lucy opened the door to find Michael, with his arms bandaged from his shoulders down to his hands, sitting up in bed, propped up with lots of pillows.

'I've come to enquire how you are,' said Lucy.

'I think I'm lucky to be alive!' said Michael.

'You need lots of rest now to get your strength back,' said Lucy.

Just then there was a knock on the bedroom door, 'Oh, bother!' muttered Michael under his breath, ' -come in!'

The door opened and Florence came in carrying a small tray with a glass on it. 'Mrs Brookes said it was time for you to have your medicine.'

Michael took the glass from the tray but could not bend his arm to drink from it.

Lucy said, 'Let me have the glass,' and turning to Florence, said, 'will you go down to the kitchen please and ask Mrs Plum for a straw so Michael can take his medicine?'

Shortly afterwards, Mrs Brookes came into the room, '-I'm very sorry Michael, the thought never crossed my mind that you could not bend your arm. If you would like Lucy to hold the glass, you can drink your medicine through a straw.'

'I hope it tastes nice!' said Michael, bending his head towards the straw.

For the next few seconds Michael's face said it all, 'UGH!' said Michael, 'that was awful!'

Lucy and Mrs Brookes were having a job not to laugh at Michael's reaction and the face he had pulled.

'Never mind Michael, you've only got to take it once a day!' said Mrs Brookes. 'I shouldn't stop too long, Lucy, Michael needs all the rest he can get.'

'Please stop a little longer, Lucy, -it's lonely being here on my own.'

'Well, not too long then!' said Mrs Brookes, as she left the room.

Next morning, Mrs Brookes was talking to his lordship in the hall, when she saw Lucy coming out of her room.

'Lucy, Michael has been asking for you.'

'How is he this morning?' enquired Lucy.

'Well, he's had a good night's sleep,' said Lord Barnes, 'and seems a lot more cheerful this morning. Perhaps you would go up to see him.'

When Michael saw Lucy, he said, 'I'm glad you have come. I begin to feel a little better and should like to know how the party arrangements are progressing. Perhaps you will tell me? I think you have been helping Mrs Brookes with it?'

'Yes,' said Lucy, 'I'm sure all will be ready when the day comes.'

'Well, that's good news. I have been told by my father that I must keep around the Manor for a while. When I can get up and walk around downstairs, perhaps you would show me some of the things my father brought back from his travels? -the ones you have been recording.'

'Yes, I will,' said Lucy, 'but what has given you this sudden burst of energy, Michael?'

'I don't know!' said Michael.

'Perhaps it was the medicine?' suggested Lucy, with a chuckle.

Michael laughed. 'Perhaps it was!'

As the days passed, Michael was allowed downstairs. He and Lucy were often seen together. It was clear they were wanting to be in each other's company as much as they could. Lord Barnes had noticed how Michael had changed, as he was beginning to take more interest in the running of the Estate, which pleased him. He also noticed how much time Michael was spending with Lucy. This was not a bad thing he thought.

It was the day before Michael's birthday party, and everyone was busy at the Manor getting ready for the big day. Several Estate workers arrived to set up the tables in the Great Hall. Mrs Brookes had asked for help in putting up the decorations, and Mrs Plum had extra help in the kitchen with the food preparation. While all this was going on, the Police Inspector arrived to see his lordship, and was shown into the study.

'It is thought the man who attacked your son is still in the area,' the Inspector said to Lord Barnes. 'I think it wise if one of my officers is present at the Manor tomorrow, just in case of any trouble. He can mingle among the guests, and be on hand if needed.'

'I will remind my son to stay around the Manor today.

He seems to have other interests at the moment anyway, if you know what I mean?'

A broad grin appeared on the Inspector's face.

'Oh, to be young again!' he said.

'It's a good thing as it keeps him around the place more!' replied Lord Barnes.

'By the way,' said the Inspector, '-your Mr Parry has asked me to investigate a light being seen every now and then at the Old Gatehouse. Your housekeeper reported it to him.'

'That's been empty for a long while,' said Lord Barnes. 'Let me know if you find out what's going on there Inspector.'

'I will keep you informed, my lord.'

CHAPTER 6

The day of the birthday party arrived. His lordship was one of the first to wish Michael a happy birthday, closely followed by Mrs Brookes, but the one person Michael was waiting to see hadn't arrived at work that morning.

'Where's Lucy?' Michael enquired.

'She hasn't arrived yet,' said Mrs Brookes, looking worried. 'It's most unlike her to be late. I will find out where she is.'

One of the Estate workers was sent to Lucy's home to find out what had happened. On his return, he reported that she had left for work at the usual time that morning.

'Whatever could have happened to her?' Lord Barnes was very concerned, and ordered the grounds around the Manor to be searched in case she was unwell or had had an accident on her way to work.

An hour or so went by and still there was no sign of her.

Lord Barnes said, 'In view of what happened to Michael, we cannot wait any longer. I will contact the Inspector and let Lucy's mother know everything is in hand. I hope nothing has happened to her.'

Word soon got out of Lucy's disappearance. People in the village were asked to let the police know if they had seen anything unusual. Michael was especially worried.

Just before lunch, the Inspector arrived to see his lordship.

'We have made several inquiries, my lord,' said the Inspector. 'No one has seen her. I can only assume Lucy has been abducted.'

'But why?' said Lord Barnes.

'I'm not sure,' said the Inspector, '-although it could be a way of getting back at your son. They have been seen together quite a lot lately. I'm going to ask for more help in order to check every building in the village. Perhaps your lordship would do the same with the buildings on the Estate?'

'I most certainly will,' said Lord Barnes.

A thorough search was then made of all the out-buildings around the Manor.

'What about the Old Gatehouse?' said Mrs Brookes to Mr Parry, who had just popped in to give his lordship an update on how things were going.

'I will have a look there just in case,' said Mr Parry.

When he arrived at the Old Gatehouse, he noticed some of the grass had been trodden down and looked as if something had been dragged over it. On closer inspection, he saw the back door of the kitchen had been forced. He pushed it open and went inside, calling out, 'Is there anyone there?' He thought he heard something in one of the other rooms, and on going further into the house, he was surprised to see Lucy laying on the floor of the dining room, tied up and gagged.

'Lucy!' cried Mr Parry, 'Oh my girl, am I glad to see you!'

Running over to where Lucy was, he quickly removed her gag and untied the ropes that held her. Helping her to her feet, he asked, 'Are you alright?'

'Yes, I think so, thank you,' said Lucy, looking a little pale and rather shaken up, though brushing the dust off her clothes as if nothing had happened. 'I hoped it would not be long before someone would find me!'

Just then, one of the policemen who had been asking questions in the village, appeared. Seeing Mr Parry and Lucy, he said, 'Are you alright, miss? We've been looking for you everywhere.'

'We must get you back to the Manor straight away,' said Mr Parry.

'-And I must inform the Inspector you have been found,' said the policeman.

Mr Parry helped Lucy out of the Gatehouse towards his pony and trap.

'They will all be glad to have you back, especially Michael!' said Mr Parry. 'Do you know who did this to you, Lucy?'

'Yes, I recognised his voice, -it sounded like Felix, his lordship's man-servant-that-was. Although he was wearing a mask over his face, I'm pretty sure that's who it was.'

When they arrived at the Manor, they were met by Lord Barnes, Mrs Brookes and Michael.

Lucy was escorted into the hall where the Inspector was waiting.

'First of all,' said the Inspector, 'do you wish to go with Mrs Brookes to clean up?'

'Oh, yes please,' said Lucy, '-the floor in that room wasn't very clean!'

Mrs Brookes took Lucy upstairs. Meanwhile, Lucy's parents had been informed that she was safe, and told they could come to the Manor to see her. One can imagine the relief felt by all. As for Michael, he was overjoyed at seeing Lucy safely back, because secretly he was beginning to fall in love with her.

After a short while, Lucy reappeared with Mrs Brookes and was able to relate to the Inspector and Lord Barnes all that had happened that morning. The Inspector said he was aware that an organisation with foreign influence was currently active in the area, and that this man, Felix, was probably mixed up with them.

'But why should he take it out on your son or Lucy?' he asked.

'We had a disagreement a little while ago,' said Lord Barnes. 'He tried to blackmail me, so I gave him his marching orders! He's a nasty piece of work.'

'As I approached the Old Gatehouse on my way to work, I thought I saw someone in there so I went to have a look. Suddenly, someone sprang out at me and dragged me inside,' said Lucy.

'The sooner we catch this man, the better,' said the Inspector. 'Meanwhile, will you keep all your staff away from the Old Gatehouse today? -Just in case he returns tonight to see Lucy, -though I rather think he will have heard that she has been rescued, and won't dare to come near.'

During the afternoon, guests started to arrive at the Manor for Michael's birthday party.

'Have you seen my son, Mrs Brookes?' said Lord Barnes.

'Ah, I think you will find him with Lucy, my lord,' replied Mrs Brookes, with a smile. 'Would you like me to go and fetch him?'

'Yes please,' said his lordship. 'He ought to be here to greet the guests now that they are beginning to arrive.'

'It's a good thing we got things forward yesterday,' thought Mrs Brookes, as she made her way to find Michael, '-after what happened with Lucy this morning, we would have been in a fix, there's no doubt about it.'

When Mrs Brookes entered Lucy's room, she was taken aback at finding Lucy and Michael in each other's arms.

'Now then,' said Mrs Brookes, '-there's plenty of time for that later on! Michael, your father is looking for you. It's time to greet your guests.'

'Thank you, Mrs Brookes,' sighed Michael, letting go of Lucy reluctantly.

When they entered the Great Hall where the birthday party was to take place, they found some of the guests already waiting. As soon as they saw Lucy and Michael, they all cheered and wanted to know about Lucy's recent ordeal.

Shortly afterwards, once all the guests were in their places, Lord Barnes made a short speech, thanking everyone for coming, and for all the help given in the recent search for Lucy.

'Now I want everyone to enjoy themselves, so have a jolly good time!'

There was food aplenty and liquid refreshment too.

'I've never seen so much food!' remarked one of the guests. 'Lord Barnes has certainly done his son proud.'

After the meal was over, the tables were taken away and the Great Hall was made ready for dancing. While all this was being done, the musicians were setting up and tuning their instruments. Finally everything was ready, the music began and the dancers took to the floor.

'It's a spectacle to behold!' remarked Mrs Brookes. 'The ladies in their party dresses and the gentlemen in their Sunday best are a sight to see!'

As the evening progressed, more refreshments were served, and by the time it was midnight and the dancing came to a halt, everyone said what a lovely party it had been. As the guests started to leave, Lucy's father thought that they ought to be on their way too, especially since Lucy had had such an eventful day.

'I must just say goodnight to Michael and his lordship,' said Lucy.

'Well, don't be long, you know I've got to be up at six o'clock tomorrow morning for work!' said Lucy's father, with a smile.

It was a rather hurried goodnight, (which disappointed Michael, who had been looking forward to a longer one!) - but still, he was most relieved that Lucy was safe and unharmed.

CHAPTER 7

The morning after the party, things moved a little slower than usual.

Father and son were in the study when the Police Inspector arrived to ask Michael some questions about the days when his mother was alive. Michael found this extremely unsettling.

'Well,' he said, 'I had a younger brother, and one day, when my mother had taken us to the seaside for a holiday, we both went swimming in the sea. Unbeknown to me, my brother was having difficulties and was swept out to sea by the strong current. Although a search was carried out along the coastline, his body was never found. I don't think my mother ever got over it. She had to go away after that, -I suppose she had been admitted into a Home, and my Aunt Carry looked after me. It was several years later, when we were staying in the hotel where, unbeknown to me, my father was also staying, that someone came into my room at night and tried to smother me with a pillow. Luckily for me, a man going past my door heard me shouting for help and came to my rescue. It was thought at the time that my father was implicated in some way, but thankfully the person who came to my aid was able to give a description of my attacker to the police. As for my mother, I am not quite sure of her whereabouts at that time, all I knew was that she had been moved into another Home. More recently, my father and I have tried to find out where she might have been taken, but no one has been able to help us yet.'

'Thank you,' said the Inspector. 'It must be hard on you to recall the past.'

'I'm sorry I can't tell you any more than that,' said Michael.

'Well, if the Inspector has finished with you,' said Lord Barnes, observing his son's distressed face, 'why don't you go and find Lucy? I'm sure she will be pleased to see you.' Michael didn't want telling twice. He made his way out of the study and across the hall to find her.

Seeing him in such an unhappy state, Lucy said, 'Why don't you show me the presents you received for your birthday?' But Michael was in no mood to look at presents. Instead, he said he would rather go for a walk with her in the gardens.

Next day, Mr Parry came to the Manor to see his lordship. Mrs Brookes showed him into the study where Lord Barnes was going through the Estate's accounts. After spending an hour or so with his lordship, Mr Parry told him that the Inspector had given him clearance to have the door of the Old Gatehouse kitchen repaired, and that he was going to send Mr Jolly, the carpenter, to see to it.

'I don't think Mrs Brookes has seen any more lights at night at the Old Gatehouse,' said Mr Parry.

'No, I haven't heard of anything being seen there,' said his lordship. 'I gather from the Inspector that he is as puzzled as we are as to what exactly is going on.'

It was about two weeks later, as Lucy was crossing the hall, that she saw a young lad standing there, dressed in his Sunday-best suit and holding a cap in his hand.

'Can I help you?' asked Lucy.

'I'm waiting for Mr Parry to take me in to see his lordship,' said the young man. 'I've come for a job, but Mr Parry was called away just as we got here.'

Just then Mrs Brookes appeared. 'Is anything wrong?' she enquired.

'No,' replied Lucy. 'This lad has come to see his lordship about a job. He came to the Manor with Mr Parry but he has been called away.'

'Yes, I know,' said Mrs Brookes. 'Come with me, young man - I will take you in to see his lordship.'

When Lucy walked into her room she had a nice surprise. Michael was there waiting to see her. He immediately put his arms around her and kissed her passionately. Lucy set all thoughts of self-control aside as she hoped the moment would go on forever!

'Will you be my wife?' asked Michael, 'because I love you so much, and have for some time.'

'Oh, Michael, I do love you too, but it's not long since my eighteenth birthday and we will have to get my parents' consent,' replied Lucy, 'of course I will marry you!'

It must have been lunchtime before the two of them reappeared holding hands. They went to see his lordship to ask for his blessing. Lord Barnes congratulated Michael on his choice of a wife, -a young woman he knew would make his son very happy. Ever since Lucy had started working at the Manor, Lord Barnes had thought she would make someone a good wife one day and was delighted his son had come to the same conclusion, although a little surprised it was so soon.

'Now I must go and see your father, Lucy, to ask his permission to marry you,' said Michael.

'I think you will find him as pleased as I am!' smiled Lord Barnes. 'George Fanshaw is one of my oldest friends -he will be delighted.'

'Lucy, when do you think would be the best time to see your father?'

'I should think after lunch. You will be sure to find him in the glasshouse,' said Lucy. 'He said this morning that that's where he would be working today.'

Lucy's parents were as delighted as Lord Barnes at the news, and were thrilled to see their only daughter so very happy.

News soon got out about the young couple. Now that they were engaged, Lucy and Michael no longer had to hide their affection for each other when in company. They had to think about their future together and where they would like to live. Lucy knew it had to be somewhere nearby because Michael was helping to run the Estate.

'What about the Old Gatehouse?' said Michael, a few weeks later.

'Oh, that place hasn't got happy memories for me!' said Lucy. 'But I must say, while I was prisoner there, it filled in the time to imagine how the room might once have looked, -I knew it wouldn't be long before someone found me.'

'Well, what do you think? Shall we have a look at it then?' said Michael.

'Alright,' said Lucy, somewhat reluctantly.

'We had better ask father if that's all right. It hasn't been lived in for many years and may need too much doing to it.'

After Lord Barnes had given his approval, they made their way down the drive to the Old Gatehouse. For a while, they just stood and looked at the place, trying to imagine what it would be like to live there.

'Let's go inside,' said Michael, taking the bunch of keys out of his pocket.

They made their way to the front door, which Michael had difficulty in unlocking. Eventually he managed to open it. When they got inside, they found themselves in the hall with doors on the left and right, and as they walked down towards the far end, Lucy said, 'That's the room where I was held.' She then went on to tell Michael how she would arrange things if it were hers.

'There's plenty of dust and cobwebs about!' remarked Michael, 'but I must say, I'm pleased to see the ceilings are quite high. In these old houses, the ceilings can be very low.'

When they went upstairs, Michael lost no time in taking advantage of the opportunity to give his future wife a kiss or two, in fact they spent quite a while there!

Coming downstairs, Lucy said, 'My mother told me that when the last family lived here, they really looked after the gardens, and were always winning prizes at local shows for their fruit and vegetables. I know they lost their little girl while they were here, but if the place was cleaned up and decorated, and the gardens made to look nice again, I think we could be very happy here. It has a warm feeling about it!'

They made their way out of the back door. As they walked around the house they came to a detached building.

'What's in here?' enquired Lucy.

'I think it might be the wash-house,' said Michael, 'or something like that. I remember my father telling me about it when I first came here and he was showing me pictures of the Estate.'

'Let's have a look inside!' said Lucy.

Michael tried to open the door but it was locked. Taking out the bunch of keys, he attempted to unlock it.

'That's funny!' said Michael, '-not one of these keys will open it. I expect the lock has been changed or maybe it's broken. I will have to see Mr Parry about it.'

As they walked further round, they passed another door on the other side of the wash-house.

'What's in here?' enquired Lucy.

'It looks like the place where firewood and coal are kept,' said Michael.

'This could be made a lovely place to live,' said Lucy, looking around, 'provided something is done down there by the lake to make it safer.'

As they neared the water's edge, Michael said, 'It looks as if someone has been down here recently, in fact the path up to the house seems to have been used several times, as if someone has been going back and forth. I must see Mr Parry right away about this.'

When they arrived back at the Manor, Mrs Brookes told them that Lord Barnes and the Police Inspector were waiting for them in the study. As soon as Lord Barnes saw Michael, he said, 'How did you get on looking around the Old Gatehouse?'

'We quite like it,' said Michael, 'and we wondered if we could live there when we are married. I know it wants a lot of doing up, but it would be handy for getting to and fro from the Manor. We have had a good look, and think we could be very happy there, but there is definitely something odd going on right now…The path down to the lake has been used a lot, and when I tried to open the door to the wash-house, none of my keys fitted. Has it had a new lock?'

'Not to my knowledge!' said his lordship.

It was then that the Inspector entered the conversation.

'I would be pleased if what I'm going to tell you was treated in the strictest confidence. I suppose now that Lucy is going to marry your lordship's son, it's safe to let her in on what I'm going to say. She has already been involved in a way which is connected. It has been confirmed,' went on the Inspector, 'that there is an organisation out to discredit this country. It is run by a group of terrorists with foreign attachments, and we believe they have been holding their meetings in the wash-house of the Old Gatehouse. They must have replaced the original lock with one of their own, so they could come and go whenever they wanted. That's why Mrs Brookes has seen lights there on a few occasions. I'm going to ask you all to keep away from there until we have apprehended those responsible. The place is under surveillance. That Felix chap is also mixed up with them, and we now know it was he who attacked you Michael, as well as abducting Lucy. I shall keep you informed, your lordship, of our progress. It shouldn't be long before we catch them.'

When the Inspector had gone, Michael said to his father, 'Are you sure it will be alright for us to live in the Old Gatehouse? You know it will need a lot doing to it.'

'Of course it is, my boy,' said his lordship. 'As soon as I get the all-clear from the Inspector, we will ask Mr Parry to accompany us down to the house so he can organise cleaning the place up. You can tell him how you want things, and you can have it refurbished however you both wish.'

CHAPTER 8

It was at the end of that week on the Friday night, just as Mrs Brookes was going to bed, that she saw lights again down at the Old Gatehouse. As she stood watching, a lot more lights appeared and as she looked out of the window, she observed even more coming up the drive towards the Manor. Next she heard loud knocking on the front door. Mrs Brookes hurried downstairs. On opening the door, she saw the Inspector and one of his Constables.

'Come in,' said Mrs Brookes.

'Is his lordship still up?' asked the Inspector.

'Yes, I think he is. I'll go and fetch him,' said Mrs Brookes.

Making her way across the hall, she saw Lord Barnes coming down the stairs in his dressing gown. When he saw the Inspector standing there, his lordship asked them all to follow him into the study.

'I'm sorry to disturb you at this time of night, my lord, but I thought you would like to know that we have been successful in rounding up the gang that have been holding their meetings down at the Old Gatehouse. After tomorrow you can have the building back. I know your son is anxious to start doing the old place up.'

'Yes,' said his lordship, 'he will be pleased. Thank you, Inspector, for letting me know. Perhaps you will call on me tomorrow and fill me in with all the details?'

'Indeed I will, my lord. Well, we must be going and let you good folk get to bed,' said the Inspector.

Following his lordship up the stairs, Mrs Brookes said, 'I'm very glad that's all over now.'

'So am I,' said his lordship.

Next morning, when Michael sat down for his breakfast, his father told him about the late night visitors, and broke the good news that they could now start to get the Old Gatehouse looking nice again.

'I think we should have a word with Mr Parry about getting things underway, but first, I should like you to come with me to the farm. Nigel Blair has a lame horse he wants me to have a look at,' said his lordship.

Just before they left to go to the farm, Michael managed to see Lucy, who was busy in her room.

'I've got to go with my father to the farm to look at a lame horse. I won't be any longer than I can help. -I have something to tell you,' said Michael. Just then he heard his father calling. '-Blast! -I shall have to go!' Giving Lucy a kiss, he went to join his father who was waiting for him in the hall.

When Michael arrived back, he went to see Lucy to tell her the good news about their future home. Meanwhile, Lord Barnes asked Mrs Brookes to see him in the study.

When she came in, he said, 'I have to go away on a little holiday, and I would like to take Michael with me. Do you think I'm being unkind to Lucy, separating them for a couple of weeks just now that they have got engaged?'

'It's a funny thing,' said Mrs Brookes, 'Lucy was saying only the other day, that an old school friend has asked her to go and have a few days' holiday by the sea, but she was concerned that Michael would think she wanted to get away from him. In fact, he's all she talks about at the moment!'

'I think I had better have a word with both of them,' said his lordship, 'and let them decide themselves what they want to do. Now that the police have cleared the area of those villains, we can get on with life. When you next see Michael and Lucy, will you ask them to come and see me?'

'I will,' said Mrs Brookes.

During the afternoon, Michael went to find Lucy in her room and said, 'My father wants to see us both as soon as possible in the study.'

'What's he want to see us about?' enquired Lucy.

'I don't know,' replied Michael.

'Let's go and see,' said Lucy. She always got on very well with his lordship, and Lucy thought perhaps it would be something to do with their engagement.

When they arrived, Lord Barnes said, 'I am going away for two weeks' holiday and I would very much like you, Michael, to come with me. How do you both feel about that? I understand from Mrs Brookes that you, Lucy, have been invited to spend a few days away with an old school friend. I don't want to stop you both seeing each other, -it's nothing like that,' said his lordship, 'I just think it would be nice for me to spend some time with my son on his own, before he gets married. Meanwhile it will give Mr Parry and his men a chance to clear much of the rubbish out of the Old Gatehouse garden, and get the dust and dirt out of the house, so that when we return, you both can start making the place your own.'

Lucy was the first to speak, by saying she thought it would be lovely for his lordship to have his son with him on holiday '-though I shall miss you dreadfully, Michael.'

'-And I shall miss you too, Lucy.'

'Well,' said Lord Barnes, 'there's still a few days before we will be leaving, so if you, Lucy, can arrange to visit your friend at the seaside while we are away, you won't be so lonely.'

The two lovers left the study feeling as though the bottom had fallen out of their world.

'Whatever shall I do without seeing you for two weeks?' said Michael.

'I feel the same,' said Lucy.

Just then Mrs Brookes, seeing them leaving the study, came over to say that Cook had just been baking, so why not come down to the kitchen for a nice cup of tea and a piece of cake? Michael accepted and they all made their way to the kitchen.

Next morning, Lord Barnes asked Michael and Lucy into the study to help him arrange the holiday. Lord Barnes thought this would help Lucy to feel part of things, and she would know where her intended would be while they were apart.

'I won't be going as far away as you, Michael,' Lucy said, 'only as far as the East coast, and then only for a week.'

A few days passed, and the time came for Lord Barnes and Michael to set off on their travels. Lucy knew that saying goodbye to Michael was going to be hard, so she must try to be brave when the time came. Standing on the steps by the front door of the Manor, she and Mrs Brookes waved goodbye to his lordship and Michael. With tears in her eyes, she turned away so that Mrs Brookes didn't see, but Mrs Brookes was feeling emotional as well, and putting her hand on Lucy's shoulder, the two women embraced. 'There, there,' said Mrs Brookes, 'he will soon be back.'

'A whole two weeks,' sobbed Lucy.

'The time will soon slip by -especially if you keep busy,' said Mrs Brookes, recovering her composure.

Nonetheless, time dragged for Lucy during the next few days until it was time for her holiday. Freda commented to Mrs Plum that Lucy was like a fish out of water since Michael went away. As for Michael, he hardly spoke a word to his father until they boarded the boat for France, and then it was, 'I hope Lucy is alright.'

CHAPTER 9

Two weeks passed, and the day came when Lord Barnes and Michael were due home. Lucy was at work early that morning because she wanted to be there when they arrived. Mr Parry had gone to meet the train and bring them both back to the Manor.

Mrs Brookes and Lucy stood outside on the front steps when Mr Parry drew up. Michael leapt out, and flung his arms around Lucy, kissing her as he did so.

'Oh Lucy, I have missed you!' said Michael, with tears in his eyes,

'-and I have missed you too,' said Lucy.

Turning to greet Lord Barnes, Mrs Brookes said, 'Welcome back my lord. Shall we leave the young ones to recover while we go inside? Have you had a nice holiday?'

'Yes, thank you,' said his lordship, 'we have had marvellous weather. The sun shone every day, -in fact I think I've caught the sun on my face! What's the weather been like here?'

'Not too bad for this time of year,' replied Mrs Brookes. 'How was Michael while he was away?'

'He was very quiet at first,' said Lord Barnes, 'but when we boarded the boat he seemed to brighten up. I hope he has enjoyed his holiday. How was Lucy?'

'Well, we had a few tears when you left,' replied Mrs Brookes, 'but she soon got over it, and now they are both catching up on lost time by the looks of it! You will find the post on your desk, and now I'll let Cook know that you have both returned.'

Later on, Mrs Brookes saw Michael on his own. She said, 'You look as if you have had a good holiday, Michael.'

'Yes, thank you, Mrs Brookes, it was nice to spend time with my father, but I'm glad to be back.'

For Michael and Lucy, much of their spare time was spent down at the Old Gatehouse whenever opportunity arose, giving Mr Parry instructions as to how they would like the rooms decorated. They also requested that the area around the bottom of the garden be made safer by fencing off the lake, but leaving access to the jetty at the end of the path by fixing a gate there. Mr Parry was pleased to be getting the Old Gatehouse up and running again, and Lucy's father was involved with providing plants and rose trees from the glasshouses on the Estate for his daughter's garden. The timing could not have been better as it was late summer, and so much could be done at this time of year.

As work started on the fence across the bottom of the garden, one of the farm workers, who had been assigned to dig holes for the fence posts, came across some stone foundations about eighteen inches below the surface. When Mr Parry was told about this, he came over to investigate.

'Try digging another hole,' said Mr Parry, 'we'll see whether it's a large lump of stone or the foundations of a building then.'

A second hole was dug just as Mr Parry had instructed, and as soon as the hole was about eighteen inches deep, they came across another large stone.

'There must have been a wall here at one time,' said Mr Parry. 'Leave off digging here for the moment, while I go and have a word with his lordship.'

On hearing about this, Michael was intrigued and wanted to find out more, so he went in with Mr Parry to see his father.

'I don't know of any building ever having been there,' said his lordship. 'I will look at the plans of the Estate to see if any mention is made of something there in the garden. Meanwhile, stop any further work in case we have to move the line of the fence.'

The newspaper announcement of Michael and Lucy's engagement aroused a certain amount of interest, and the fact that, at last, the Old Gatehouse was being renovated, made the villagers speculate when the wedding was going to be. A picture of the Old Gatehouse also featured in the same paper, as it did in other country periodicals.

A few days later, Lord Barnes and Mr Parry were discussing what progress had been made with the house itself, when his lordship reported that he had looked through the plans of the Estate, but could not find any reference to there being a building of any sort at the far end of the garden.

'I know the place is very old, so maybe there could have been something there before the Gatehouse was built. I have to go to London on Friday, so I will make a few enquiries while I am there,' said his lordship.

'Well, I must go and see how things are at the house,' said Mr Parry, 'when I last saw it, they were putting the finishing touches to the outside.'

On arrival at the Old Gatehouse, he found Lucy and Michael inside making a list of things that they had to buy for the kitchen.

'Is everything alright, Michael?' enquired Mr Parry.

'Yes, it's fine thank you,' replied Michael. 'Have you been able to find out anything more about the foundations at the bottom of the garden?'

'No, I haven't yet,' said Mr Parry. 'Your father is going to London on Friday, and while he is there he is going to make inquiries to discover whether there was ever a building on that site.'

'Everything is beginning to look lovely,' said Lucy to Mr Parry. 'We both thank you for all the time and trouble you have taken in making this house so nice for Michael and me. We are very grateful.'

'It's a pleasure!'

Mr Parry returned to his office to write a report for his lordship on the work being done at the Old Gatehouse. This included new slates on the roof, new gutters, new pointing around the chimneys, and the removal of a very vigorous ivy, making progress up one of the outside walls. As far as the garden was concerned, it required a complete overhaul, as much of the original planting and shrubs had died, leaving only weeds. There were a few old apple trees, but as they hadn't been pruned they were only useful as firewood. When Mr Parry had finished writing his report he took it over to the Manor for his lordship.

When Friday arrived, Lord Barnes sent for Michael and told him that he might be in London for several days, as he intended making enquiries about the area where the stone foundations had been found.

'I've told Mr Parry not to let anyone work in that part of the garden until we know something further.'

When his lordship had left, Michael went to Lucy's

room to ask her if she wanted to go with him down to the house to see how things were progressing.

'Your father told me that if I needed any time away from work to go to the shops, I was to take it,' said Lucy, 'so I am going to go shopping with my mother this morning.'

'That's alright,' said Michael, 'I will see you when you get back.'

As Lucy was leaving her room, she met Mrs Brookes.

'Just going out?'

'Yes,' said Lucy. 'I'm meeting my mother and we are going shopping.'

'Can I come?' said Mrs Brookes, jokingly.

'If you would like to!' said Lucy, smiling.

'Perhaps another day,' said Mrs Brookes, '-well, have a nice time, Lucy!'

CHAPTER 10

Michael had just finished his breakfast when Lucy went into the dining room to see him.

'How did the shopping go?'

'My mother bought me a new dress, and I've something for you, Michael,' said Lucy, handing over a parcel covered in silver wrapping paper.

'I wonder what's in here?' said Michael.

When he had unwrapped the parcel, he exclaimed, 'A pair of gloves! -Just what I was wanting,' and taking Lucy in his arms, he kissed her.

At that moment Florence entered the room to clear the breakfast things away.

'Oh! I'm sorry, I'll come back later,' said the flustered maid.

'You can clear the table, we are just going,' said Michael. Taking Lucy's hand, they both left the room.

'I ought to have my coat if we are going down to the house,' said Lucy.

'I will get it for you,' said Michael.

When they arrived at the Old Gatehouse, they both stopped and looked at what was going to be their new home.

'Just think,' said Lucy, 'I never imagined when I lay tied up in one of those rooms, that I would be living here one day!'

'We are going to make it just how you want,' said Michael. 'What you like, I know I shall like as well.'

Taking Lucy's hand they both went inside.

As they entered the kitchen, Lucy mentioned she had seen a very nice dresser in a shop and thought it would go very well in there.

'My father has told me that we can buy whatever we like for our house, and he will see it is paid for.'

'That's very kind of him,' replied Lucy. 'We're very lucky.'

It was almost a week before his lordship returned. On being met by Mrs Brookes at the front door, Lord Barnes asked where both his son and Lucy were.

'I think they are in Lucy's room my lord. Shall I go and fetch them?'

'If you would, Mrs Brookes. Thank you.'

'Come in,' said Lord Barnes, when he saw Michael and Lucy at the door. 'I have news for you. After making enquiries at several places in London, I finally discovered what might have been at the bottom of your garden. It has been suggested that the stone foundations are part of a burial site.'

'Ugh!' shuddered Lucy.

'-and it is thought that a Norman lord might be buried there, but we can't be sure. There used to be a stone cross to mark the place where the grave was, but of course, that has long since gone. We have the choice of moving the fence line and leaving things alone, or we can investigate to see what's there. How do you feel about it?'

'I don't like the thought of living in the house with someone buried in the garden,' said Lucy.

'That's how I feel,' said Michael, 'I think we should go ahead and find out.'

'Very well,' said Lord Barnes, 'I will inform Mr Parry to go ahead.'

'I should like to be there when they start to dig,' said Michael.

'I think we must keep it to ourselves at the moment,' said Lord Barnes, 'otherwise we will have a lot of onlookers.'

The next day, Mr Parry and some of the workforce from the farm arrived to start digging. After about an hour, they uncovered what seemed to be the floor of a building, and with further investigation, saw it was covered in mosaic.

'This looks like the remains of a Roman building!' exclaimed Mr Parry.

'I must go and tell father,' said Michael.

When Lord Barnes heard the news, he hurried down to see what had been found.

'There's not a lot of it,' said Mr Parry to his lordship, 'but when it is cleaned, we will be able to see how much mosaic there is.'

'I must go and fetch Lucy,' said Michael, 'she will love to see this.'

'This discovery has been worth all our time and expense,' said Lord Barnes, 'we must make a feature of this, and preserve it as long as we can. Mr Parry, can you erect a temporary cover over the mosaic so it is kept dry, and is not open to the weather?'

'I can,' said Mr Parry.

'When you have seen to that, will you come up to the Manor to report to me?'

'Yes, my lord,' replied Mr Parry.

As soon as Lord Barnes, Michael and Lucy were back at the Manor, his lordship asked, 'Do you mind having this mosaic at the bottom of your garden? We can't cover it up now we have discovered it, can we?'

'No,' said Lucy, 'I don't know what Michael thinks, but as long as we don't have lots of sightseers trampling over our garden, as far as I am concerned, I think we must keep it. What are your thoughts Michael?'

'I am in agreement with you,' replied Michael. 'I was thinking a little way ahead -after we are married and perhaps have children, we must consider their safety in what we decide now.'

'Quite right, Michael,' said his lordship. 'I was thinking of some form of cover, perhaps a low structure erected over the mosaic which would keep it dry, and prevent little people from falling in!'

'That seems to be the answer,' said Lucy.

'Very well,' said his lordship, 'I will see to it right away.'

CHAPTER 11

Just over a week later, Lord Barnes called Michael into the study.

'I have heard from the architect and he has sent me a drawing of the roof needed to cover the mosaic at the bottom of your garden. If you like it, we can give Mr Parry instructions to proceed. The sooner a permanent roof is put in place, the better.'

'Can I show this to Lucy?' said Michael.

'Yes, by all means,' replied his lordship. 'Once Mr Parry gets the drawing, he can start work.'

Michael lost no time in seeing Lucy, and after talking

it over, they delivered the drawing to Mr Parry. As there were men employed in the workshops on the Estate, it didn't take long to produce a suitable structure and erect it over the mosaic in the garden.

'With a few rose trees planted around, it will make a nice feature,' remarked his lordship.

A few days later, Michael said to Lucy, 'I think Mr Parry has seen my father regarding the wash-house. He asked me whether we would like it joined to the kitchen if it can be done, so we don't have to go outside in the bad weather.'

'It would certainly save the kitchen staff several steps as well,' replied Lucy.

'By the way, Lucy, have you given any thought to the staff we shall need? It is only a three-bedroomed house so perhaps it would be possible to put another bedroom, or even two, on top of the wash-house if they do manage to join it to the kitchen? I will have a word with my father about it if you agree? The only thing is, we shall have to wait to be married in the Spring in order for the work to be carried out first. How do you feel about that?'

Lucy was in agreement and suggested Michael go in to see his father right away. Giving Lucy a parting kiss, Michael left the room.

The door to the study was open and Michael saw Mr Parry there.

'Come in!' said his lordship. 'This is fortuitous! I have asked Mr Parry here to talk about your idea for modernising the wash-house and building a bedroom or two over the top. Have you spoken to Lucy about this yet?'

'Yes, we have just been talking about it - it makes good sense.'

'Well,' said Mr Parry, pointing to his drawing, 'I have already looked at the possibility of more rooms down at the Old Gatehouse, and if we join the wash-house to the kitchen side of the house, we may well finish up with enough space to make two bedrooms on top. We could make a doorway from inside the kitchen, through the new extension to the wash-house. If we move the outside doorway round the corner next to the woodshed door, we could build a porch to extend over both doors and you would have protection from the weather when it was time to fetch in the coal for the fires.'

'I can see you have been doing your homework, Mr Parry. I know it's up to Michael and Lucy to decide, but I am in total agreement. It's an excellent idea.'

'Yes, it is!' agreed Michael. 'Lucy will be pleased, and although it's later than we had intended, it will mean we can have a Spring wedding.'

'I think the three of us should go down to the house to look,' said his lordship, 'and if all is well, I will forward the plans to the architect for his approval.'

'I have the trap outside, my lord, -would that be alright?'

'Yes,' said his lordship, 'just let Mrs Brookes know where we are going, Michael, and tell her we won't be long because I have a meeting later on this morning and I don't want her thinking I have forgotten!'

Michael made his way to Lucy's room, expecting to find Mrs Brookes there, but instead he found Lucy on her own, so, going over to her, he took her in his arms and kissed her. After a short while he said, 'Oh, blow! I have a message for Mrs Brookes from my father.'

'I will tell her,' said Lucy, 'I'm going to see her shortly.'

'Well,' said Michael, 'will you tell her that my father and I are going down to the Old Gatehouse with Mr Parry, and that he will be back for his meeting later on this morning.'

At that, Michael went to join his father and Mr Parry.

Lucy found Mrs Brookes down in the kitchen, talking to Mrs Plum and Freda, and delivered the message from his lordship.

Later that afternoon, Michael, who had been discussing the work to be done at the Old Gatehouse with his father, made his way to Lucy's room.

'Will you stay for dinner tonight?' enquired Michael, 'then we can go for our usual walk in the grounds first.'

'I'd love to!' said Lucy, 'but that will be the third time this week! My mother looks forward to my coming home after work, but lately she never sees me! As for my father, he says he had a daughter once, yet almost forgets what she looked like! But I know my father, -he's an old tease! They are both pleased for us and hope we will be very happy together.'

'So will you stay for dinner then?'

'Of course!' smiled Lucy.

'I will let Mrs Brookes know,' replied Michael.

A little later, Michael and Lucy went out into the gardens for their walk.

'Don't the dahlias look lovely?' remarked Lucy.

'Yes, your father has spent a lot of time nurturing them, -the chrysanthemums too. They all look splendid,' said Michael.

As they walked along among the flowers, Michael stopped and swung Lucy round, embracing her and kissing her, 'Oh Lucy, Lucy, I do love you.'

'-And I do love you too, Michael, but I think it would be wise if we went out of the garden as the kitchen windows look out over here and we can be seen from the Manor!' remarked Lucy. 'Let's go over towards the park -there are seats there and we can sit and enjoy the last of the evening sunshine.'

'Have you noticed,' said Michael, 'that the benches which have been placed for people to sit on, are all sited in a private position? When I was with Mr Parry in our garden, he asked me if we would like a seat placed by the lakeside. When I made a suggestion as to where it could go, Mr Parry said, 'I shouldn't put it there, I think this would be more private,' and so I agreed. I think our Mr Parry is a bit of a romantic as he said 'you're only young once!' -But don't let's talk about him, -has anyone ever told you what lovely hair you have, Lucy?'

Kissing her soundly, Michael whispered hoarsely, 'I do love you so, my lovely wife-to-be.'

After some little while, Lucy remarked, 'Oh, look Michael! The harvest moon is just rising above those trees, everything is so peaceful - I could stay out here with you forever, but I think we ought to go in to dinner now, and I mustn't be quite so late getting back tonight, because I'm getting a few black looks from my father when I arrive home. He always waits up for me.'

'Well, at least it shows he cares for you. I'll say this for your dad, he and his team of gardeners keep the flower and vegetable beds in first class order at the Manor, and I believe he has had more than a hand in the planting of flowers and fruit trees at our house?'

'Yes,' said Lucy, 'he asked me what we would like in our garden, so I told him what we had decided.'

'I hope your dad will still keep an eye on our garden when we are living there, because I haven't got a clue!' said Michael.

'I'm sure he will,' replied Lucy, kissing him on the cheek.

CHAPTER 12

The next day, just before lunch, Lord Barnes sent Florence to find Michael, who was supposed to be helping Lucy! When Michael entered the study, his father showed him a letter he had received that morning. It was from an old friend of his lordship's, Professor Clifton. In it, the Professor said he had been on holiday abroad and whilst reading a magazine, learned of the discovery of the mosaic at the Old Gatehouse. He was interested to know whether anything else had been unearthed at the site, since it was usual for there to be a small chamber either nearby or even beneath a mosaic floor. There was a possibility it could be the remains of a Roman building or villa.

'Well!' said Michael to his father, 'we had better keep this to ourselves until we can decide what to do for the best. Lucy will be excited.'

'I think we should have a word with Mr Parry, and put him in the picture,' said his lordship, '-just in case he noticed anything odd while they were uncovering the mosaic, but I don't think we should do anything further at the moment.'

'What about the wash-house extension and bed-rooms?' asked Michael.

'Oh, that's alright,' said his father, 'they can go ahead. I will ask Mr Parry to come to see me this afternoon -you can be present if you wish?'

'Yes, I do,' said Michael.

During the afternoon, Mr Parry arrived to see his lord-ship and was shown into the study.

Lord Barnes and Michael were already there, waiting for him.

'Come in,' said Lord Barnes, 'we have something interesting to tell you. But first, how are things progressing with the wash-house?'

'Most of the materials we need are on site,' replied Mr Parry. 'We may have to strengthen the walls of the wash-house as we extend them to the kitchen wall, but we will have to dig the foundations for the extension first. I have seen the architect and he has approved the plans already.'

'That's good,' said Lord Barnes. 'Now then, I have received information regarding the mosaic at the bottom of Michael's garden. It appears there might be more there than we have already discovered, but I do not want it investigated at the present time, -let's get the extension over first. Did you notice anything unusual when the mosaic floor was being uncovered, Mr Parry?'

'I did notice that the walls supporting the floor seemed to go down in the ground a long way, but as we were working against time, I thought no more about it.'

'Well,' said his lordship, holding up the letter, 'Professor Clifton thinks there could be a chamber under the mosaic. It will be an interesting project, but we have quite enough on at the moment getting the extension finished before the bad weather sets in. We must have a chat about all that later.'

When the meeting was over, Michael went to tell Lucy all about it.

'My father won't be very happy if the garden has to be dug up again,' said Lucy, 'he has spent a lot of time there making everything look nice for us.'

'I know he has,' replied Michael, 'but nothing is going to happen until the extension is complete, and then we will have a meeting with my father and Mr Parry to see what's best to do.'

The next day, the front door bell rang. On going to see who was there, Mrs Brookes was surprised to see the Inspector standing on the doorstep.

'Could I have a word with his lordship?' asked the Inspector.

'Yes,' replied Mrs Brookes, 'I think he is free.'

'Isn't it a grand morning?' said the Inspector as they made their way to the study door.

'Come in,' said Lord Barnes.

'Thank you,' replied the Inspector. 'Well, my lord, what I have to tell you will surprise you. It concerns your younger son. After listening to Michael telling us about his brother being drowned all that time ago, and the fact that the boy's body was never found, I checked up on some of our files relating to that time. Just along the coast from where the accident happened, is the port of Harwich where the boy's body could have been picked up by the crew of a ship. But a body was never reported. If he survived, then why hadn't he been in touch? It all seemed such a mystery. Well, the good news is that somebody was picked up just about that time, by a ship going to a port in the Far East, and I am waiting to hear from one of our men sent out to investigate the case. As soon as I hear anything, I will let you know.'

'Heavens above! I can't believe what I'm hearing,' said his lordship. 'I was away when it happened and only know what Michael has told us. His brother would be a year younger than Michael and his name was William Charles Barnes. I can't thank you enough for all the trouble you are taking. What are the chances it could be my son?'

'It's too soon to say, my lord, but I will keep you informed.'

As the Inspector left the study, he saw Mr Parry waiting to speak to his lordship.

'Good morning, Mr Parry!'

'Good Morning, Inspector!'

'Come in,' said his lordship to Mr Parry, 'I have just been given some very good news. -At least, I hope it is, -the Inspector is going to let me know. Now, how are things progressing down at the wash-house?'

'We started to dig the foundations for the extension between the wash-house and the kitchen, but we came across a brick floor. When we started to remove the bricks, it all collapsed and we were left with a hole in the trench. It looks as if we have broken into a large water course or sewer. I thought I would try to lower a light on a rope to see what we have found and I will report back to you, my lord, once we have done so.'

'That place seems to be full of surprises!' said his lordship. 'Very well, see what you can find.'

Mr Parry left for his office to look for something suitable to lower into the hole. Finding a lamp and a piece of rope, he returned to the Old Gatehouse. One of the men had already put a rod into the hole and found it went down about three or four feet. Mr Parry then lowered the lamp into the hole, revealing what looked like a tunnel. Just then his lordship arrived and Mr Parry showed him what they had discovered.

'Well, I never expected anything like this!' exclaimed Lord Barnes, 'we had better find out where the tunnel goes, but first we must make sure it would be safe for a man to go down into it. We really need a small person to go down. Let's see….' said his lordship, 'perhaps young Albert Blair is about? He's small and intelligent -just the boy!'

Speculation grew amongst the workmen as to what they would find. Mr Parry left to fetch more lamps to ensure there was plenty of light in the tunnel in case of an emergency, or should anything untoward happen.

By the time young Albert Blair arrived, Mr Parry had already had the hole made larger by removing some of the brickwork to make the operation as safe as possible.

'Down you go, young man!' said his lordship to young Albert, 'but be very careful not to disturb anything. All we want you to do is just tell us what you can see.'

Carefully, they lowered Albert on a short length of rope into the hole.

'WHEW!' said Albert, 'it does stink down here, but at least it's dry!'

Lowering the lamp down, Lord Barnes asked, 'Now, can you see where the tunnel goes to?'

'It goes down towards the lake,' said Albert. 'Shall I go along to see? There's plenty of room for me to get through.'

'No, not without a longer rope around your waist!' cried Mr Parry.

'Did you say the tunnel was dry inside?' said his lordship.

'Yes,' said Albert.

After they had tied a longer rope around Albert's waist, they lowered him back into the hole, and he set off down the tunnel, holding the light as he went. Mr Parry was talking to him all the time to make sure he was alright. As Albert crawled along, his voice became fainter and fainter. Suddenly the rope stopped moving.

'Are you alright?' shouted Mr Parry. They heard a muffled reply but could not make out what the boy had said.

'Get him out!' said Lord Barnes.

Mr Parry gave a tug on the rope and to his relief, the rope became slack as Albert started back.

When the boy had got his breath, he said, 'There was a small door at the far end of the tunnel, in the wall. I tried to open it, but I could not get hold of anything to pull it open. It was an iron door and very rusty. I was having a job to breathe, so I thought I had better get out.'

Lord Barnes said to Albert, 'You have done well, young man, I will take you back and explain to your mother why you are in such a mess, but I don't want you to tell anyone what you have seen and done. I am going to reward you for your help this morning, because without you, we might never have known what was down there.'

After Lord Barnes and Albert had gone, Mr Parry took the rope and laid it out on the ground to see how far the boy had crawled, putting a stake to mark the spot. When his lordship returned, Mr Parry showed him where he thought the tunnel ended.

'Do you remember that letter I showed you a little while ago, from Professor Clifton?' said his lordship. 'Perhaps this is what he was getting at when he referred to an article he had seen in a magazine. I think we should carry on with the work at the wash-house and leave this for the time being. Meanwhile, I will have another look in the library at the Manor, to see if I can find any reference made to a tunnel being built at the same time as the Old Gatehouse. It certainly looks as if there were buildings on this site a long time ago, and that they have since been demolished.'

CHAPTER 13

Somehow, word got out, and anticipation grew as to what would be found at the end of the tunnel. Lord Barnes had hoped to keep things quiet, but to his dismay, found a report in the local press, giving an account of how the tunnel had been discovered. He knew then to expect a visit from his more curious, so-called 'friends' in London.

Making his way down to the Old Gatehouse, Lord Barnes saw Mr Parry, and acquainted him with the newspaper article, warning him to be on the lookout for further visitors from the press. They decided that the longer they waited before the tunnel was opened up, the more chance there was of it being forgotten about.

'Now, how are things progressing with the wash-house?' enquired his lordship.

'Well,' said Mr Parry, 'as you can see, we are going to break through into the roof space of the house today.'

'I hope we don't have any more surprises!' remarked Lord Barnes, 'I've had enough surprises recently to last a life-time!'

'No,' said Mr Parry. 'I think this one will be quite straight forward!'

'The sooner the new roof is on, the better. This weather won't last much longer.'

'No, my lord. Once we have the building water-tight, we can press on inside. I thought I would put a trapdoor in the floor of the lobby, in case we want to enter the tunnel from this end.'

'That's a very good idea,' said his lordship.

Work went on inside the new extension right up to the end of November. It was then decided to leave the finishing touches until the New Year, weather permitting.

Once Christmas was over, Michael and Lucy went to see Lord Barnes to fix a date for their wedding. His lordship consulted his diary.

'When were you thinking of?'

'Sometime just after Easter, -the weather should be warmer by then!' said Michael.

'Yes, that will be ideal. Work will have finished on your house by then, and there will be plenty of time now to send out the invitations. We've dilly-dallied long enough!'

'Lucy, we will have to go and see the vicar,' said Michael.

'Ask him to come here so I can see him too,' said his lordship.

'I will,' replied Michael. 'May I suggest we have a meeting in the next week or two, with all the staff who will be involved in preparing for the wedding?'

'That's a good idea, Michael,' said his lordship. 'I will ask Mrs Brookes to arrange it.'

It wasn't long before Mrs Brookes gave his lordship a list of staff who she thought should be involved in the wedding preparations. She had already been thinking about this for a little while and was well-prepared when his lordship asked her. This resulted in his lordship, Lucy and Michael, sitting round the table the following day with six members of staff to discuss the wedding breakfast, which would be held in the Great Hall of the Manor. During the meeting, each member of staff was assigned his or her part in the preparations. Lord Barnes said that several important guests would be attending and added that those coming from a long way away would need overnight accommodation.

'I will see that all the guest bedrooms are cleaned and made ready,' replied Mrs Brookes.

'Do you think we will require extra helpers?' asked his lordship. 'If so, perhaps you would see to it, Mrs Brookes.

The next day, the vicar arrived to see Lord Barnes.

'I will fetch my son and his fiancée.'

Michael had gone to help Lucy with the wedding preparations in her room, and when his lordship walked in and caught them in each other's arms, he cleared his throat, announcing, 'The vicar's here to see us -you will have plenty of time for all that after you are married!' Lucy felt a little embarrassed at being caught out by his lordship. Together, the three of them made their way to the study.

'My lord,' said the vicar, 'I had a visit from the bishop this morning, and when I told him of Michael and Lucy's wedding, he said he would like to take part. I trust you are happy with this? Now, have you young people given any thought to the service?'

'We have chosen the two hymns we would like,' replied Lucy, 'but that's as far as we've got.'

'Perhaps now you are here, you will help us decide exactly what we do want?!' said Michael.

It took quite a while before they could all agree on what form the service should take, and they set the date for the last Saturday in April. His lordship stressed, once again, that there would be many important guests present, '-the Lord Lieutenant for one, so we must get it right!'

When the vicar had taken his leave, Lucy said, 'Michael, we could begin to make a list of people we want to invite. My mother has already started to write down names of relatives who will be expecting to receive an invitation.'

'That's a good idea,' replied Michael. 'I expect you, father, will have several of your London friends wanting to come?'

Leaving his lordship, they made their way to Lucy's room to make a start on the guest list, but Michael took advantage of being alone with his future wife, and for the next few minutes little was done in the way of wedding preparations!

During the next fortnight, the invitations to the wedding were sent out. The kitchen staff had been very busy making the wedding cake, Lucy and the bridesmaids had been for their final dress fittings with Lucy's mother, and Michael had been up to London to be fitted for a new suit, so all was going well. Michael and Lucy spent most of their time between the Manor and the Old Gatehouse, getting their home ready for when they returned from their honeymoon.

'Mr Parry has done a wonderful job here,' said Michael, 'he has carried out everything we asked him to.'

'It's not the same garden,' said Lucy, 'I know we shall be very happy here. Now, as for staff, my mother was telling me that she knows of a Mrs Craddock who is looking for work, and says we could do a lot worse than to take her on. Also, Mrs Plum's daughter has just left school, and is looking for work as a kitchen maid.'

'Well, that's a start,' said Michael, 'are they trustworthy?'

'My mother assures me that they are, and says Mrs Craddock has an excellent reputation.'

The next morning, Michael received a letter from his cousin Robert, telling him that his Aunt Carry had died suddenly, and that he hoped both Michael and Lord Barnes would be able to attend the funeral. He would let Michael know when it would be. Michael immediately went to see his father to tell him.

'This is going to be a little difficult,' said Lord Barnes. 'Next week I am expecting Colonel and Mrs Parks to stay, and Judge Fellows and his wife will be coming the day after they leave. We will have to wait and see when the funeral is going to be,' said his lordship.

Michael went to see Lucy to tell her about Robert's letter.

'I'm sorry she has died. She was very kind to me after my mother had to go into that Home. Cousin Robert and I got on very well, although we seem to have lost touch lately. It will be nice to see him again though. Perhaps after we are married, he could come and stay for a few days, Lucy?'

'Yes, of course, Michael, -that would be very nice,' said Lucy, putting her arm round him. 'I'm so sorry. From what you have told me, she seems to have been a lovely lady. Well, now I must go and update Mrs Brookes on the guest list.'

Leaving Michael, she made her way to Mrs Brookes' room. Meanwhile, Michael went back to his father to talk about the work being done at the Old Gatehouse.

CHAPTER 14

Afe breakfast the next morning, Lord Barnes was standing in the doorway of the study when he saw Mrs Brookes make her way across the hall towards Lucy's room.

'Have you seen my son this morning, Mrs Brookes?' his lordship enquired.

'No, my lord, I haven't seen him since breakfast, but I can guess where he is!'

'If you see him, will you tell him I should like to have a word?'

'Certainly I will,' said Mrs Brookes.

When she arrived at Lucy's door, she gave a little cough and tapped before entering. She saw Michael and Lucy together, and it was evident they were not discussing the weather!

'Your father is looking for you, Michael,' said Mrs Brookes, 'you will find him in the study.'

'Thank you, Mrs Brookes. Lucy and I were just talking about the wedding.'

'Of course you were, Michael!' she said, with a grin on her face.

A few minutes later, Lucy, having found another query on the guest list, went down to the kitchen to find Mrs Brookes who was talking to Mrs Plum and Freda.

'I wonder how long this lovely weather will last?' said Mrs Plum.

'I hope it stays like this for the wedding,' said Lucy.

'So do I,' said Mrs Brookes. 'There will be a lot of folk hoping this weather will last so they can wear their Sunday best for the wedding.'

'I have bought a new hat for it,' said Mrs Plum.

'-And I have got a new dress,' said Freda. 'What about you, Mrs Brookes?'

'Ha!' said Mrs Brookes, 'you will have to wait till the day.'

'I expect it will be something fetching!' said Freda, cheekily.

'You mind what you say,' replied Mrs Plum, putting Freda in her place. 'I'm sure we will all look nice on the day.'

'Will you wear a veil, Lucy?' enquired Freda.

'Yes, I will,' replied Lucy, 'but I really came down here to ask Mrs Brookes.......' Just then, the front doorbell rang.

'I must go and see who that is,' said Mrs Brookes.

Lucy, realising that Freda was in one of her inquisitive moods, took advantage of the moment to leave as well.

'Were you wanting to speak to me, Lucy?'

'Yes,' said Lucy.

'I'll be with you shortly.'

The next morning, Lucy went along to the kitchen for her mid-morning break, and found Mrs Brookes in conversation with Mrs Plum. Turning to Lucy, Mrs Brookes said, 'Were you looking for me, Lucy?'

'Yes! Who's doing the announcing at the wedding reception?' asked Lucy.

'A Mr Riddle,' said Mrs Brookes.

'Did you say 'Widdle'?' retorted Mrs Plum.

There was a shriek of laughter from Freda.

'No, -his name is 'Rrrriddle',' said Mrs Brookes. 'His lordship engaged him. I think he is coming from London especially for the wedding. I know we have got to put him up for the night. We will have a houseful then! -And that reminds me, I must have a word with Florence about bedlinen.'

After they had had their break, Mrs Brookes and Lucy left the kitchen, leaving Mrs Plum and Freda, -who was still chuckling to herself, at the sink!

A few days had passed, and guests who were staying at the Manor for the wedding, started to arrive. It looked as if the weather was set fair - at least, that was the forecast, but as Mrs Plum kept saying, 'You can never be sure!'

Extra help was on hand in the kitchen, as had been requested, and flowers were being placed all around the Hall and in the entrance to the Manor. With only two days to go before the wedding, everything looked lovely. Lucy's father had been down to the church to take flowers and greenery to those helpers who were decorating inside. -As he said, 'It's my daughter who's getting married, and I want her to have the best.'

And best there was. The vicar remarked that he had never seen the church look so beautiful.

At last, the day arrived for the wedding. There was a blue sky and it was warm, with a gentle breeze. The wedding was to be at twelve noon.

After a good breakfast, Michael went to see his father, who had asked to see him in the study.

'I'm not going to tell you how to behave once you are married, but I would ask you to always respect your wife, be kind and love her. Lucy will make you a good wife, treat her well.'

'I will, father,' said Michael, 'I love her very much.'

'I know you do, my boy,' said his lordship, 'I hope you will both be very happy together. Send me a card while you are away so I know you are alright.'

'I will, father.'

After Michael had seen his father, he went to the drawing room to find Harry, his best man.

'I wondered where you were,' said Harry. 'In an hour's time, we shall have to go to the church.'

'I wonder how Lucy is feeling?' said Michael, 'yesterday, she was so excited that the day was nearly here.'

'You're a lucky man to be marrying a lovely girl like Lucy. I envy you,' said Harry.

As for Lucy, she had breakfast with her mother and father who said proudly, 'It's not every day I give my daughter away to be married!'

'No!' said Lucy, 'I wonder how Michael is feeling this morning?'

'Probably got a hangover!' replied her father, with a grin on his face.

'His best man, Harry, and a few friends, were going to have a bit of a 'do' last night,' said Lucy. 'I do hope he's alright this morning!'

'When you have finished your breakfast, Lucy, I think it best if we get you ready slowly,' said her mother. 'I hope the bridesmaids are feeling well, - you never know with young people.'

'It looks like we shall have a nice day for our wedding,' said Lucy.

'I ordered it special!' said Lucy's father, jokingly.

'Just you wait, -when I've seen to Lucy, it will be your turn!' replied Lucy's mother, with a laugh.

The time came for Michael and Harry to leave for the wedding. Outside the Manor was a carriage and two grey horses standing ready to take them both on the short drive to the church.

When they arrived, Michael and Harry walked to their places at the front of the pews to the strains of 'Jesu, Joy of Man's Desiring' being played on the organ. As they sat there, Michael's thoughts went back to his mother, -how he wished she could have been there, and also the brother he once had. How they would have loved to see Lucy. Michael's thoughts were suddenly interrupted by a dig in the ribs from Harry.

'It's time!' said the best man.

They both stood up. Michael turned and saw Lucy looking radiant and smiling at him. She was coming up the aisle towards him on the arm of her smartly-attired father, and holding a bouquet of roses. Then followed the four bridesmaids.

'You do look lovely, Lucy,' Michael whispered, as she drew level with him. Lucy handed her bouquet to the chief bridesmaid, and then, with Michael, turned to face the vicar.

When the service was over, the happy couple walked down the aisle to the 'Wedding March' played joyfully on the organ by Mr Gray. As they made their way out of the church, the bells were ringing, and the guests were waiting to shower them with rice and confetti as they made a dash for the carriage. Taking advantage of the occasion,

Michael put his arms around Lucy and kissed her soundly, much to the delight of the guests, who cheered loudly.

After the photographs had been taken, they left for the Manor where they were met by Mrs Brookes, who congratulated them, wishing them every happiness in their lives together. After they had thanked her, Michael hoped he would be able to have a few moments alone with Lucy before the guests returned from the church, but no such luck! They soon found themselves surrounded by guests, all wanting to wish them well.

Some time later, his lordship intervened, saying they ought to let the happy couple have a chance to get ready for the reception. Michael and Lucy were relieved to be able to get away, albeit for a short while. Michael took Lucy to his room, and the two fell into each other's arms.

'Oh, Lucy, Lucy, I do love you so!' said Michael, kissing his bride thoroughly.

'-And I do love you too, Michael!'

A little while later, Lucy asked, 'Did it seem a long time before I arrived at the church? My father insisted we should be a few minutes late, as is the custom!'

'No,' said Michael, in between kisses, 'but I was glad to see you when you did arrive. I wish I could stay like this with you in my arms forever, but I suppose we had better go and join our guests now!

When they arrived in the Great Hall, where the reception was being held, they found most of the guests were seated. Once everyone was settled, a cheer went up as

Michael and Lucy made their way to the top table with his lordship and Lucy's parents.

'Cor! What a spread!' said young Albert Blair. 'I've never seen anything like this before!'

'No,' said his mother, 'nor have I. Now don't go making yourself sick!'

When all the guests were seated once more, Mr Riddle, the Master of Ceremonies, stood up and announced:

'My lords, ladies and gentlemen, pray silence for his lordship.'

Lord Barnes began by wishing his son and daughter-in-law every happiness in their lives together, and welcomed everyone to the celebrations. He went on to say how pleased he was that his son had chosen Lucy for a wife, since she was the daughter of one of his best friends, -a man he had known for a long time, even before he went abroad, and who had given faithful service to the Estate.

He also thanked the staff at the Manor, along with the Estate workers, for a magnificent effort in preparing for the wedding festivities.

'That's all I have to say at the moment. Enjoy your meal!'

After the Wedding Breakfast was over, Michael and Lucy were wanting to leave for their honeymoon, but the more they tried to escape, the more guests wanted to talk.

Finally, Lucy managed to slip away with her mother to change from her wedding dress into her going-away outfit. She appeared all smiles with Michael, and together they made their way to the front door of the Manor. As they stood waiting for their carriage which was to take them to the station, young Albert pushed his way through the guests and gave Lucy a silver horseshoe for good luck.

'Thank you,' said Lucy, giving Albert a peck on the cheek and making him blush.

When their carriage arrived, driven by Mr Parry, resplendent in coachman's livery, the young couple said their farewells. Lucy's father drew Michael aside and said, 'Look after my daughter, she is very precious to me.'

'She is very precious to me too,' said Michael. 'I will keep her safe, you've nothing to worry about.'

Waving as the carriage moved off, they made their way down the drive, past their new home and onwards towards the station.

They didn't have to wait long for the train and were fortunate to find an empty compartment. Michael and Lucy were glad to be on their own. As the train drew out of the station, Michael said, 'At last I've got you to myself! I shall always remember seeing you on the arm of your father as you walked up the aisle to be my wife. I can picture it now. You looked wonderful!'

'-And I will always remember seeing you, standing there and turning to look at me as we walked up towards you. Then we passed Mrs Plum in that big hat of hers, -with the feather sticking out, and it made me want to laugh, but I caught sight of the vicar waiting for me, with the bishop standing there in full attire too, and all thoughts of Mrs Plum's hat went out of my head! I was quite warm in my dress,' said Lucy, 'who would imagine the weather would be so lovely? Oh, Michael, I feel so happy!'

'So do I,' said Michael, putting his arms around her and giving his new bride a kiss.

As for all the guests at the Manor, they were in for a treat. His lordship had engaged musicians, jugglers and singers, and with the addition of free-flowing liquid refreshment, the entertainment was enjoyed by all! Then followed dancing, and a spectacular firework display to round off the evening.

While all this was going on, the staff at the Manor were busy clearing up from the reception held earlier in the day.

'Just look at that heap of washing-up!' remarked Freda. 'Guess who will be doing that?'

'We will give you a hand,' said Mrs Plum. 'Our two helpers will as well. I must say, Freda, your two young brothers had a good time with the chocolate cake! I hope they don't suffer for it!'

'They are a pair of rascals!' said Mrs Brookes, who had just popped into the kitchen to see

Mrs Plum. 'They're a handful, I'll be bound!'

'I wonder how Michael and Lucy are feeling?' said Mrs Plum. 'I thought Lucy looked lovely, -in fact it brought on a few tears to see them both so happy together.'

'You were not the only one to feel like that!' admitted Mrs Brookes, 'I do not think I have ever seen a bride look so radiant and happy as Lucy did when she walked up the aisle to be wed.'

Just then, Florence came into the kitchen, carrying another tray of dirty plates.

'More washing-up!' groaned Freda. 'We will never get this lot finished before Christmas!'

'What about you, Freda?' said Florence. 'When do you intend to get married?'

'I didn't know she was walking out with anyone,' remarked Mrs Plum.

'Oh, he's only just a friend,' replied Freda, colouring up.

'Oh, yes?' said Florence. 'That's not what I've been told!'

Freda, who was obviously embarrassed at what Florence had just said, turned away and got on with the washing-up.

'Well, I don't know!' sighed Mrs Plum, '-these young people!'

At that moment, his lordship appeared at the kitchen door.

'Ah, there you are, Mrs Brookes! I just wanted to say a big 'thank-you' to you and all the staff for your help in making this day such a happy one for my son and Lucy. It will be strange without them being around. Now, as it is so late, Mrs Brookes, I think it wise if the staff started work an hour later tomorrow morning.'

'Very good, my lord. Thank you,' replied Mrs Brookes.

CHAPTER 15

It took most of the following day to return the Manor to normal.

'I thought the church looked lovely,' said Mrs Brookes, when she went into the study to see his lordship. 'The flowers were beautiful.'

'Yes, I agree. George did us proud. Now, I think the Colonel and his good lady will be leaving us today,' said his lordship, 'and I've got Mr Parry coming to see me this morning, Mrs Brookes, so will you show him in?'

'I will, my lord.'

Monday found Florence and Maud busy upstairs, and

the last few rooms to be vacated by wedding guests were being given a thorough going-over.

'I'm glad we don't have a houseful all the time!' said Maud.

'So am I!' replied Florence, 'it makes a lot more work.'

'I nearly told that Colonel Parks' wife what she could do with her night-cap!' said Maud, '-you know she blamed me for pinching it? What would I want with a night-cap, I ask you?'

'I think it would suit you!' teased Florence. 'Did she find it?'

'I s'pose she must have done,' said Maud.

Just then, Mrs Brookes came into the room.

'Maud, go down to the village and fetch Dr Jones. Freda has cut her hand badly and it will need stitching, -be as quick as you can. Come with me, Florence, we are needed in the kitchen to help Mrs Plum clear up the mess.'

When they arrived, they saw a sorry-looking Freda, sitting on a chair, with her hand in bandages, and a tourniquet around her arm.

'I think we should give Freda a cup of sweet tea, -that might help to give her strength,' said Mrs Plum. 'Will you sit with her, Florence, in case Freda comes over queer? It's all my fault,' continued Mrs Plum, '-I had been slicing the meat for tonight's meal, and put the knife into the washing-up water without telling Freda. I'm so sorry, Freda.'

'That's alright, Mrs Plum. I should have been more careful when I put my hands into the bowl.'

When Dr Jones arrived, he said, 'Now my girl, what have you been up to?'

'It's all my fault!' cried Mrs Plum.

'So you're the culprit, are you, Mrs Plum?' said the doctor, jokingly. 'Let's have a look, shall we?'

Taking the bandages off Freda's hand, he said, 'Ah! This will need a little stitch to close the wound and give it a chance to heal.'

What happened next wasn't very pleasant for Freda, but she put on a brave face and the ordeal was soon over.

'Now,' said Dr Jones, 'I think it would be for the best if someone would take you home so you can have a rest. Keep the bandage on for a few days so you don't get it infected, and keep your hand out of water.'

Mrs Brookes asked Florence if she would take Freda home and explain to Freda's mother what had happened.

'We will be short-staffed in the kitchen now,' said Mrs Plum.

'Would your daughter be able to come in to fill the gap?' suggested Mrs Brookes.

'Yes, I think so,' replied Mrs Plum. 'I will ask her.'

The next day, Agnes started work in the kitchen with her mother. She had been well-schooled as to what her duties would be.

'This will be good experience for you when the time comes to apply for a permanent position,' her mother said. 'You might be asked by Miss Lucy when she returns. They will be needing staff at the Old Gatehouse.'

Three days passed and Freda was well enough to come back to work. Mrs Brookes said she could help in the house for the time being, until her hand had fully healed.

'Florence, have you seen his lordship this morning?'

'Yes, Mrs Brookes, I think you will find him in the library.'

Lord Barnes was searching through a large leather-bound book.

'I'm sorry to trouble you, my lord, but I thought you might like to have this letter as it looks to have come from Michael.'

'Thank you, Mrs Brookes. I was wondering when we might hear from him. I expect it was Lucy who told my son to write, he would have other things on his mind at the moment!'

Handing the letter over to his lordship, Mrs Brookes left the room and made her way to the kitchen, to see Mrs Plum.

'I thought you might like to know, his lordship has just had a letter from Michael!'

'It's about time!' said Mrs Plum.

'Well, they are on their honeymoon!' replied Mrs Brookes.

Just then, his lordship came into the kitchen.

'I thought you might like to know that I have heard from Michael and Lucy. They are both well and enjoying the sunny weather. Michael said they go swimming most days as the water is warm, but they have to be careful of the jellyfish.

I expect they will be quite brown when they return!'

'Thank you, my lord,' said Mrs Brookes, 'I'm glad they are having a nice time, -by the way, my lord, is it today that the furniture is being delivered to the Old Gatehouse?'

'Yes, I almost forgot!' said his lordship. 'I will go down to the house, and in any case, I want to see Mr Parry.'

'Isn't it exciting?' said Mrs Plum.

'Yes, -I have had so much on my mind about the wedding, that I almost forgot about the furniture! I told Lucy I would see to it too,' admitted Mrs Brookes.

As she crossed the hall, Mrs Brookes saw Florence coming away from the front door.

'Mrs Brookes!' called out Florence, 'there is a large furniture van outside!'

'I will see to it,' replied Mrs Brookes, and went out to give the van driver instructions. She then went to find his lordship.

The following week, Lord Barnes received another letter from Michael and Lucy, bearing the news that they would be returning on Friday of the next week. He went in search of Mrs Brookes and suggested the newly-weds reside at the Manor until their house was ready.

'They will need staff,' said Mrs Brookes.

'Yes, I know,' said his lordship. 'Have you any recommendations?'

'Lucy did mention to me that she knew of a Mrs Craddock who would be suitable as housekeeper, and

I must say, I have heard good reports about her,' replied Mrs Brookes.

'Ask her to come and see me if you would,' said his lordship.

The next day, Mrs Craddock went to see Lord Barnes. Mrs Brookes showed her into the study.

'He won't be long,' she said.

After a few minutes his lordship appeared, 'Good morning Mrs Craddock!'

'Good morning, my lord!'

'My son and his wife will be looking for staff at the Old Gatehouse. They will be needing a housekeeper. I believe my daughter-in-law, Lucy, may already have said something to you?'

'I have been asked if I might be available, my lord. I am, and I would be delighted to oblige.'

'Splendid! As regards your wages, I must leave that between you and my son, Michael. He will make arrangements for you to collect your wages from the farm office, along with the rest of the staff who work here. My son will be returning from his honeymoon on Friday, so perhaps you could be available then?'

'That will suit me nicely,' replied Mrs Craddock.

'I must leave the rest of your terms of employment to my son and his wife,' said his lordship.

'That will be alright,' answered Mrs Craddock.

'Perhaps you would like to have a word with Mrs Brookes before you go? She will be able to tell you what has been happening down at the Old Gatehouse,' said his lordship.

Getting up from his chair, Lord Barnes opened the door of the study to let Mrs Craddock out.

Seeing Mrs Brookes in the hall, Lord Barnes called her over.

'Mrs Craddock has accepted the position of house-keeper at the Old Gatehouse. Could you let her know what has been happening there, regarding the work at the wash-house?'

'Come with me,' said Mrs Brookes, and they both walked down the hall to Mrs Brookes' room.

'If you would like to sit there, I will see about a cup of tea for us both.'

As Mrs Craddock sat there waiting for Mrs Brookes to return, she looked around and thought how fortunate she would be to be working for such a well-established family. Mrs Brookes soon returned, carrying a tray with cups and saucers and a large teapot.

'Have you been a housekeeper before?' enquired Mrs Brookes.

'No,' replied Mrs Craddock. 'Since my husband died, I have been living alone, which isn't very nice, and I feel I could be helping someone and at the same time have company around me.'

'In that case,' replied Mrs Brookes, 'if there is anything you would like to know, I would be only too willing to help you.'

'That's very kind of you, Mrs Brookes. As a matter of fact, there are several things I should like to know about.'

After half an hour, Mrs Craddock went on her way, a much happier person, and with the knowledge that she had found a friend who would help her, if needed, when she began her housekeeping duties.

CHAPTER 16

The day arrived when Michael and Lucy returned from their honeymoon. They were met at the station by Mr Parry, and on arrival at the Manor were greeted with cheers from the staff.

Lord Barnes was very pleased to see them back.

'I would like to have a word with you both sometime today, -also with you, Mr Parry, but first I would like to hear about your travels,' said his lordship.

'If you come with me,' said Mrs Brookes, 'I will show you to your room, and then I would also like to have a word with you both about staffing at your new house.'

'It's nice to be back!' exclaimed Lucy, 'and to be sleeping in your old room, Michael!'

'It's only until you are able to live at the Old Gatehouse,' said Mrs Brookes. 'I have seen Mrs Craddock, Lucy. She seems a friendly sort, and I'm sure you will both get on well together. It's her first time as a housekeeper, so if you can bear that in mind to start with, I know you will find her a great help.'

'We shall also need a kitchen maid,' said Lucy.

'Yes,' replied Mrs Brookes. 'Agnes, -that's Mrs Plum's daughter, has been helping out in the kitchen here, so if you are in agreement, I think she might be suitable for you. Have a word with Mrs Craddock, -but for now -welcome back!'

After lunch, Michael, Lucy and Mr Parry met with his lordship in the study.

'It may surprise you both,' said his lordship, 'that while you were away, the workmen digging the foundations for the wash-house extension came across a brick-built tunnel. We found out it went down the garden as far as the spot where the mosaic was discovered, and what is more, there is a small door in the end wall, but we don't know what lies behind it yet. That's as far as we have got with it.'

'As for your house,' said Mr Parry, 'we have just about finished. There is only some painting to complete on the woodshed door, and then we can clear the site of tools etc.'

'There's one more thing, -and I don't hold out much hope at this stage,' said his lordship, 'I had a visit from the Police Inspector. He said that after what you, Michael, had told him about losing your brother while swimming on holiday, he decided to make some enquiries.

Apparently, someone had been rescued from the sea by the crew of a ship sailing to a Chinese port. That was several years ago. The Inspector has sent a man to try and find out what happened to the person who was rescued, but so far he hasn't heard anything. If it was William,' continued his lordship, 'surely we would have heard something from him? Nonetheless, I told the Inspector to make sure every effort was made to further the investigation, and that no expense was to be spared.'

For a moment Michael was speechless. Turning to his father he said, 'Is that all we know? What are the chances of it being him after all this time?'

'I'm afraid that's all I can tell you at the moment,' said his lordship.

Seeing how Michael was affected by this, Lucy took his hand and said, 'We must wait to see what the investigations reveal, Michael. Meanwhile, isn't it exciting about the tunnel? Oh, but does this mean that the garden has got to be dug up again to find out what's there?' asked Lucy, thinking of all her father's hard work.

'No' said his lordship, 'in the passage between the kitchen and the wash-house, Mr Parry has fitted a trap-door over the entrance to the tunnel, so we can go down any time we like without being seen from the outside. This new electric light, which I am thinking about having installed, could be very useful when the time comes to investigate what is there, but we must tread carefully with all this. Now I think Mrs Craddock will be waiting to meet you both, so I mustn't detain you any longer.'

Mrs Craddock was in the kitchen, sorting through boxes of cutlery ready to go in the dresser, which had yet to be put in place.

'Good morning, my lady,' said Mrs Craddock.

'Good morning to you,' said Lucy, being taken aback by being called 'my lady'.

'It looks as if we may want some help in putting the heavy furniture in place,' said Mrs Craddock, 'but before then, perhaps you would let me know where things are to go?'

'I will see to it,' said Michael, coming in from the garden. 'I'm Lord Barnes' son, Michael, and you must be Mrs Craddock, our housekeeper?'

'I am indeed, my lord,' replied Mrs Craddock.

Giving Mrs Craddock a big smile, Michael said, 'Oh, please call me 'Mr Michael' and my lovely wife, 'Miss Lucy', it's what we're used to.'

After pleasantries had been exchanged, Lucy said 'Shall we have a look at the new extension Mr Parry has built, Mrs Craddock?'

Lucy opened the door from the kitchen into the passage, through to the wash-house.

'I think Mr Parry has moved the door in here, so that the outside door is next to the door of the woodshed.'

Opening it, they found Mr Parry had not only done that, but built a porch over the two doors as well.

'He's thought of everything!' remarked Lucy.

'It will certainly keep everyone dry in the wet weather!' replied Mrs Craddock. 'Now, I understand Mrs Plum's daughter, Agnes, is going to be the scullery maid.'

'That's right,' said Lucy. 'We have also got to find a cook, and I think we shall need a housemaid to look after the bedrooms to start with. Mrs Craddock, I will leave you to look around and to let me know when you find someone suitable. My husband will get Mr Parry to take care of the furniture being put in place, and that small room at the back will do nicely for his study.'

'There's always a lot to do when setting up house for the first time,' said Mrs Craddock, 'but with help from Mr Parry, it shouldn't take too long to get straight now you are both back.'

The following day, Lucy said to Michael, 'I hope Mrs Craddock has remembered to contact Nigel Blair at the farm regarding the milk and butter we shall need.'

'It is Mrs Craddock's job to see to that,' said Michael, 'but we could go to the farm this morning and see Nigel

Blair anyway, and I can show you the dairy where the butter is made.'

Making their way across the meadows, they came to a small copse. In it, they saw a large mound of earth covered with grass. On one side was an opening with a door and a large window. When Michael opened the door, Lucy saw two young girls busy at work, one turning the handle of a large wooden churn, the other, patting into shape a small lump of butter.

'Good morning, ladies!' said Michael. 'We have come to see Nigel Blair. Is he about?'

'No, my lord, we haven't seen him this morning. Why don't you try the farm?'

'Very well, we will,' replied Michael.

'Brrr… It's cold in here!' said Lucy. 'Can we go?'

'Yes, it has to be cold to keep the milk and butter cool. Let's be on our way.'

As they made their way past the stables, Michael said, 'This is where I keep my horse. One of the farmworkers looks after him for me. Most of the other horses are at work on the land. There's always a lot to do at this time of the year.'

Finally, they found Nigel Blair examining one of the binders, which had broken down and was awaiting a new part.

'Good morning, Nigel!' said Michael. 'We thought we would let you know that Lucy and I will soon be living at the Old Gatehouse. Mrs Craddock is going to be our housekeeper, so she will be contacting you soon, regarding our requirements for dairy produce.'

'Very good,' replied Nigel Blair. 'I was just having a look at this binder - it's in a right mess! That will be a job for a wet day!'

Leaving Nigel Blair still pondering over his problem, Michael and Lucy returned to their house, only to find Mrs Craddock giving a red-faced farmworker a ticking off for walking across the kitchen floor with dirty boots on! He had just delivered a load of logs from the farm, and was looking out for Mrs Craddock to let her know.

'I spent all yesterday-' went on Mrs Craddock, 'trying to tidy up this kitchen, when this morning, Cloth Ears here, walks in with his dirty boots right across the floor!'

Trying not to laugh, Lucy said, 'Never mind Mrs Craddock, I think you are doing very well in getting the place ship-shape.'

Standing in the doorway, with a bemused expression on his face, Mr Parry said, '-And I shall be bringing Estate workers with me this afternoon to put the furniture in place, Mrs Craddock.'

'Make sure they wipe their boots then!'

'I will!' said Mr Parry, with a grin on his face.

CHAPTER 17

During the afternoon, Lord Barnes decided to go for a ride to inspect the two fields of wheat, since he had been concerned about them earlier on in the year. When he arrived, he found Nigel Blair there too.

'Is everything all right, Nigel?' asked his lordship.

'Yes, my lord. I thought I would check to see all was well. I think we should have a good return from these two fields this year, by the looks of it!'

'I'm pleased about that!' said his lordship. 'Well, I will be on my way, Nigel.'

Making his way back to the Manor, his lordship thought he would make a detour to see how things were progressing at the Old Gatehouse. Taking a short-cut through the woods, his horse stumbled, throwing him to the ground. Fortunately young Albert, Nigel Blair's son, was in the woods at that time and saw what happened. Running over to his lordship, he enquired how Lord Barnes was.

'Can you help me to get up?' said his lordship, looking rather dazed.

Albert, although small for his age, was a strong lad. Getting hold of Lord Barnes, he managed to get him up on his feet.

'Ouch!' said his lordship. 'I think I have hurt my ankle. Can you fetch my horse and I will try to get on it?'

Leaning against a tree, he waited for Albert to bring the horse over, managing to remount with the young lad's help.

'I think it would be better if I led you back to the farm, my lord. -That's the nearest place to get help.'

'Very well,' said his lordship, '-it was a good thing you saw what happened, I might have lain there for hours.'

As they drew near to the farm, one of the farm-workers saw them coming, and seeing things were not right, came running over to find out what had happened. Turning to young Albert he said, 'You go and fetch help. I will stay with his lordship.'

It wasn't long before help arrived, and Lord Barnes was carefully taken off his horse and conveyed back to the Manor. Michael and Lucy had been told, and were there already when Lord Barnes arrived. Mrs Brookes had sent for the doctor, and thinking it best for his lordship to rest in bed, had already made the necessary preparations.

A short while later, the doctor came, and after examining the ankle, said his lordship had sprained it.

'A few days rest and he should be fine!'

'Is that all the doctor said?' Lucy asked Mrs Brookes later, when the doctor had gone.

'Yes,' replied Mrs Brookes. 'Doctors never tell you much.'

Lord Barnes asked Michael to cancel a meeting he had been due to attend on Monday, and to make his apology, also to see that young Albert was justly rewarded for his help.

'I don't know what I'd have done if he hadn't been there.'

'Can I come in?' called Lucy to Lord Barnes.

'Yes, come in,' replied his lordship.

'How is your ankle feeling now?' enquired Lucy.

'It's a little easier now the doctor has strapped it up,' said his lordship. 'That's good,' smiled Lucy.

Michael and Lucy stayed a while with Lord Barnes, talking about how things were progressing down at the Old Gatehouse.

'I've yet to find a cook,' said Lucy. 'I have asked Mrs Craddock to look out for one.'

'Now there's a woman I should not like to cross!' remarked Michael. '-The way she went for young Brian down at the house yesterday…'

'What happened?' asked his lordship.

'Before you tell your father, please excuse me, I must see Mrs Brookes about something,' said Lucy.

'Well,' continued Michael, 'young Brian delivered a load of logs to the house, then went inside the kitchen to tell Mrs Craddock. He had just come from the farm, his boots were muddy and Mrs Craddock told him off in no uncertain terms for making a mess.'

'I think you have got yourselves a good housekeeper there, my boy,' laughed his lordship, 'look after her.'

Lucy found Mrs Brookes telling Mrs Plum and Freda all about his lordship's mishap.

'It's a good thing it's nothing worse than a sprain,' remarked Mrs Plum, 'he could easily have broken a leg falling off a horse! Lucky young Albert was there to help his lordship!'

Lucy said to Mrs Brookes, 'I've left Michael talking to his lordship. While he is confined to his bedroom, his lordship will want to know how things are on the Estate. I know Mr Parry will also keep his lordship informed, but it's nice for Michael to have time with his father, and to be able to discuss the running of the Estate, which one day, albeit a long way off, will be Michael's responsibility. They seem to get on very well together.'

'Yes, they do,' replied Mrs Brookes. 'When you come to think about it, a lot has happened since the day you started work here, Lucy.'

'Yes, I found the items his lordship brought back from abroad fascinating, especially the things in the upstairs rooms,' replied Lucy, '-and I understand from Michael that his lordship is now thinking of having the electric light installed here at the Manor.'

'I have found the telephone useful since we had it put in,' said Mrs Brookes. 'If we have electricity as well, it will save time and give us much better light to see with.'

'I think I had better go and find Michael now,' said Lucy. 'Can I have a word with you tomorrow about staffing please? It's later than I thought, and Michael and I must go and help Mrs Craddock back at the house. There's still a lot to do.'

On her way up to his lordship's bedroom, Lucy met Michael coming down the stairs.

'I was just coming to find you!' said Lucy. 'Is your father alright?'

'Yes, he wants to have a nap now. I think he is tired from talking too much!'

As they made their way out of the Manor, they met Mr Parry, who was coming to give an update on the day's happenings.

'I have just left my father -who by now, might be fast asleep, -you can but try!'

CHAPTER 18

When Lucy and Michael arrived at the Old Gatehouse, they found Mrs Craddock and Agnes upstairs, getting the bedrooms ready.

'These are nice sized rooms,' said Mrs Craddock.

'Yes,' replied Lucy. 'I think the room we are in now will have to be our room, Michael - what do you think?'

Michael nodded, then turned back to look out of the window.

'Have you had any luck in finding us a cook, Mrs Craddock?'

'Yes, I have,' answered Mrs Craddock. 'A Mrs Judd will be coming tomorrow morning for an interview with me.'

'Splendid!' said Lucy.

'Is it right his lordship has had a fall?' enquired Mrs Craddock.

'Yes,' replied Michael. 'He fell off his horse and sprained his ankle, but he should be alright after a few days in bed to rest it.'

'I'm glad it was not anything worse than that,' replied Mrs Craddock.

When they had finished looking round the house, Michael said, 'Lucy, I have something to show you in the garden.'

Making their way towards the gate which led on to the lakeside, he said to her, 'Close your eyes and take my hand.'

Holding Lucy's hand, he led her through the gate and a little way along the path. Then he stopped and said, 'You can open your eyes now!'

There in front of them was a shelter with a seat inside, facing the lake. 'I asked Mr Parry if he could arrange to have a seat put here so you and I can come and be on our own.'

'What a lovely idea!' exclaimed Lucy. 'We shall be able to sit here and watch the sun go down over the water.'

The following morning, Mrs Judd arrived at the Old Gatehouse to see Mrs Craddock regarding the position of cook. After a short and friendly chat, Mrs Craddock said, 'Let me show you round.'

'I was still at school when the last family lived here,' said Mrs Judd. 'They lost their little girl in a drowning accident.'

'Yes, I know,' replied Mrs Craddock. 'Mr Parry has had a fence put across the bottom of the garden to stop anything like that happening again.'

'Wasn't it here where they caught those men?' went on Mrs Judd.

'Yes, they were using the old wash-house to hold their meetings,' replied Mrs Craddock.

'Mr Michael has had that side of the house modernised, by having two extra bedrooms built on top of the wash-house and lobby. Now we can walk through without having to go outside. A shelter has been put over the outside doors as well.'

'Fancy that!' replied Mrs Judd.

'I have arranged the furniture in the kitchen, as you can see,' said Mrs Craddock, 'but if you want to change anything, do so. This is your kitchen now, Mrs Judd.'

'That's a nice dresser,' remarked Mrs Judd.

'Yes, Miss Lucy saw that while out shopping with her mother. You will have Mrs Plum's daughter, Agnes, to help in the kitchen. I think you will find her very willing, she has been well trained by her mother.'

'Will Mr Michael and Miss Lucy be staying here tonight?' asked Mrs Judd.

'No, they hope to start living here tomorrow,' said Mrs Craddock. 'They will be sleeping up at the Manor tonight.'

After lunch, Michael went upstairs to see his father.

'Come in!' said Lord Barnes. 'I want to have a chat about a number of things. First of all, I think it would be a good idea if we had the telephone connected to your study at the Old Gatehouse. Also, I have been making enquiries regarding having electric light installed here, -would you like it at your house?'

'Yes, please,' said Michael. 'It would be a great help for the staff not having to fill oil lamps. We must keep up with the times!'

'Quite so.' replied his lordship. 'It's a few years since the old Queen died, -how time has flown! The electric light company wants to put poles across our land, so I have asked them to give us a date for a meeting to discuss what is involved. I will get Mr Parry to sit in on the meeting too, I expect there will be a certain amount of upset while it is being done, but I want to keep abreast of things.'

'Having the electric light will be much safer than oil lamps and candles,' said Michael.

Michael left his father and went to find Lucy, who was talking to Mrs Plum in the kitchen. They were discussing how Agnes was settling in at the Old Gatehouse.

'There you are!' he said.

'I was just asking Mrs Plum about her daughter, Agnes, -our new kitchen maid,' said Lucy.

'I'm having a job to keep up with who's who!' said Michael, jokingly. 'I think we shall have to hold a roll-call each morning to see if everyone's present!'

Taking Lucy's arm, he led her out of the kitchen along to see Mrs Brookes, who was in her room.

'We will be taking up residence in our own house tomorrow, Mrs Brookes,' said Michael. 'I understand everything is ready for us to move in now, so tonight will be our last night here.'

'It will be strange not having you both around all the time,' remarked Mrs Brookes, 'but I know you will come and see us when you can.'

'We will,' replied Lucy.

Leaving Mrs Brookes, they made their way out into the garden to see Lucy's father, who was working there.

'We shall be living in our own house tomorrow, Dad,' said Lucy '-so will you tell Mum please?'

'I will,' replied Lucy's father. 'You will be needing some produce from here no doubt?'

'Yes, please!' said Lucy. 'I expect Mrs Judd will be contacting you about that. Anyway, thanks again, Dad.'

As they walked down towards their new home, Lucy asked, 'How did you get on with his lordship this morning?'

'My father is going to have the telephone laid on in my study, -also, we are to have a meeting with the electric light company when a time can be arranged. It will make a huge difference in the house if we have it installed.'

'Can the Estate afford it?' enquired Lucy, '-what with the wedding, the telephone and now the electric, it must be expensive.'

'Well, we shall see,' said Michael. 'My father knows what he is about. He has a card up his sleeve: they want to put poles to carry the wires across our land, so no doubt a deal will be made!'

CHAPTER 19

After breakfast, Michael and Lucy went up to see his lordship in his room.

'We've come to thank you for having us stay here while our house was being renovated.'

'You don't have to thank me,' said his lordship, 'it's been lovely having you both here, I shall miss you. By the way, I have heard from the electric company. They would like to see us on Wednesday at eleven o'clock, here at the Manor.'

'That's good, we'll be here,' said Michael, 'but we must be on our way now, as we have one or two things to do before tonight!'

'Look after your ankle,' said Lucy.

'I'm getting up today!' replied his lordship. 'It's much better now.'

On the way back, Michael said, 'My father will be glad to be up and about again, he hates being laid up in bed, though I think it will be a little while before he gets on a horse!'

'Tonight will be our first night in our new home,' said Lucy.

'I know,' replied Michael, 'and we won't be having Mrs Brookes hovering around, asking if everything is alright!'

'She means well,' said Lucy. 'I have always found her very kind and helpful.'

'I suppose we will be having Mrs Craddock instead!' replied Michael with a laugh. 'I wouldn't want to upset her!'

Lucy laughed. 'You will have to mind what you say to her or she might put you in your place!'

Later on, after supper, Lucy said to the housekeeper, 'It's been a lovely early summer's day, and it's so nice to have the lighter evenings, but you've had a busy time, Mrs Craddock, don't you think you ought to be on your way home now?'

'Yes, I must,' said Mrs Craddock, 'it's been quite a day! Agnes will be here first thing tomorrow morning and I have left her instructions as to what she has to do before I arrive.'

'Thank you, Mrs Craddock,' replied Lucy. 'We'll see you in the morning.'

The next day, Michael and Lucy were awakened by Agnes, knocking on their bedroom door.

'Come in,' yawned Michael.

The door opened and a rather flushed Agnes came in, carrying a tray with cups and saucers.

'I've brought your early morning cups of tea.'

'Thank you, Agnes, put the tray down there,' said Lucy.

When Agnes had left the room, Michael turned to Lucy, and taking her in his arms he said, 'I could stay here like this all day.'

When Lucy could speak, she replied with a laugh, 'I think Mrs Craddock would have something to say about that!'

When they came down for breakfast, -albeit a little late, Mrs Craddock remarked on the weather by saying it was windy out and there was talk of rain later on!

It must have been an hour afterwards, when they had finished eating, that news reached them to say that Florence had been attacked on her way to work that morning. Michael, knowing his father was still incapacitated, said, 'I must go up to the Manor immediately to see if there is anything I can do to help.'

On arrival at the Manor, Michael found the police sergeant in conversation with his lordship.

'Come in, Michael,' said Lord Barnes. 'The sergeant was just telling me about this morning's happenings. A week ago, a man named James Watt escaped from Manton

Prison, where he was serving a ten year sentence for committing grievous bodily harm for attacking young women. He has been breaking into people's houses looking for food, and now he has attacked Florence on her way to work this morning. Luckily, Florence was able to kick out where it hurts a man most, -if you know what I mean, which left him doubled up in pain. He will no doubt try again if we don't catch him. I have advised Mrs Brookes to tell all the staff to be on the lookout for this man, and from now on, until this man is caught, no-one goes out alone. It will make things a little difficult, but safety comes first. Meanwhile, Michael, you must tell Lucy, -and also Mrs Craddock, all about it. I will let Mr Parry know so he can tell the farm workers to keep a sharp eye out for this man.'

'Where is Florence now?' enquired Michael.

'She is with Mrs Brookes. She will be alright once she has got over the shock of it, but it's not nice for a young girl,' said his lordship.

'People like that want putting away for life,' remarked Michael.

'I think I will be on my way now, your lordship,' said the police sergeant. 'If the young lady should remember anything else, perhaps you would get in touch?'

'I will,' remarked his lordship.

When Michael returned home, he told Lucy and Mrs Craddock what had happened to Florence that morning.

'I know what I would do if I ever got my hands on him!' said Mrs Craddock.

'I think we all feel like that!' replied Michael.

'Now, -young Agnes,' said Lucy. 'Can we arrange it so she walks with her mother when she comes to work?'

'I will see to it,' replied Mrs Craddock.

News of the attack on Florence soon spread. The game-keepers were told to keep a sharp eye open, because it was thought the man was hiding out in the woods on the Estate. Only a few days went by when the man struck again. This time he attacked a young village woman in her own home. Luckily her husband returned in time, but was unable to overpower him and he got away.

When Lord Barnes heard about the second attack, he contacted the Inspector of Police and asked him if he would come to see him.

Meanwhile, down at the Old Gatehouse, Mrs Judd and Agnes were busy getting the wash-house ready.

'Is there a cellar below here?' enquired Mrs Judd, when Mrs Craddock came to see how they were getting on.

'Not that I know of,' said Mrs Craddock.

'-Only I noticed that trap door in the floor out there in the lobby,' replied Mrs Judd, who was an inquisitive type.

'I will ask Mr Michael when next I see him,' said Mrs Craddock, 'but I haven't been told exactly what is under there.'

Just then, Lucy came into the wash-house to speak to Mrs Craddock.

'Is everything alright?' she asked.

'Yes, Miss Lucy, -would you perhaps be able to tell us what is under that trap door in the lobby please?'

Lucy was surprised by this question at first, but then she said, 'I think they found a large hole or well there when they were building the extension, and rather than fill it in, Mr Parry thought it best to put a cover over it. If it is a well, it might come in useful later on. It's quite safe to walk on!'

'Oh, that's alright,' said Mrs Craddock. 'Cook asked me and I didn't know, so I thought I would enquire. By the way, Miss Lucy, your father has sent us some lovely vegetables. Cook remarked she hadn't ever seen finer.'

'I must thank him next time I see him,' smiled Lucy, 'now I must go and find Michael!'

When Lucy arrived at Michael's study, she found him busy doing a drawing of what looked like a wall with a door.

'That's funny!' said Lucy, 'Mrs Craddock has just asked me what was under the trap door in the lobby.'

'You didn't tell her about the tunnel?' enquired Michael.

'No,' replied Lucy. 'I said there was a large hole or well there, and rather than fill it in, Mr Parry had put a trap door over instead.'

'Oh, that's alright then,' said Michael. 'Now, when we go down the tunnel we shall need plenty of light, and it will have to be done when all the staff are away, because if there is some sort of treasure hidden down there, we don't want everyone to know about it.'

'I shouldn't think the air is very nice in the tunnel, -but it's still very exciting,' said Lucy.

'The fewer people who know about it, the better,' said Michael.

'Has anyone seen what is behind that door in the wall?' said Lucy.

'No,' replied Michael. 'When young Albert went down the tunnel he couldn't open it.'

'I hope he has kept quiet about it,' said Lucy.

'My father told him not to tell a soul about what he had seen, or where he had been.'

'Can he be trusted?' asked Lucy, 'he's very young.'

'Yes,' said Michael, 'I think so.'

CHAPTER 20

B ack at the Manor, Mrs Brookes called up the stairs
to Florence, 'Is Maud with you?'

'Yes!' called out Florence.

'Will you ask her to see me in my room in ten minutes?'

'Very well,' replied Florence.

'I wonder what she wants?' said Maud. 'I hope it's
not the sack! I can't think why Mrs Brookes would want
to see me.'

'There's only one way to find out,' said Florence, jokingly, '-go and see her.'

Maud made her way down to Mrs Brookes' room.

Knocking on the door, she heard, 'Come in!'

When she was inside, Mrs Brookes continued, 'Now Maud, I believe you have a sister a year or two younger than you, am I right?'

'Yes, Mrs Brookes.'

'Is she looking for work?'

'As a matter of fact she is,' said Maud. 'My mother was saying she wondered if Miss Lucy would be wanting a housemaid at the Old Gatehouse.'

'That's right, she is. What is your sister's name?'

'It's Lilly,' replied Maud.

'Very well,' said Mrs Brookes, 'I will let Mrs Craddock know, then she can get in touch with your mother concerning a possible job for Lilly at Miss Lucy's.'

'Thank you, Mrs Brookes,' replied Maud.

When she returned upstairs, Florence enquired about the purpose of her visit to see Mrs Brookes.

'My sister, Lilly, may be offered a job as a housemaid at the Old Gatehouse with Miss Lucy,' said Maud. 'She will be very pleased, -only last night my mother was saying it would be good if Lilly could get work at the Old Gatehouse, because Miss Lucy and Mr Michael have always been kind to me. They are two very nice people.'

'They are,' said Florence.

'Have you two finished up there?'

'That's Mrs Brookes!' said Florence. 'Yes, Mrs Brookes, we were just coming!'

'There's never a dull moment!' remarked Maud, '-what's up now?'

'I wonder,' said Florence.

When the Wednesday morning came, Michael, Lucy, Lord Barnes, Mr Parry and two gentlemen from the Electric Supply Company met in the study at the Manor. After the formal introductions had been made, Mr Jones, the Area Manager, said his company had been approached to provide power to a town on the other side of the Estate, several miles away, and since Caiston Manor was situated en route, the company had prepared a plan to supply electricity to the Manor. Lord Barnes said, 'I do not want to see a lot of poles and wires spoiling the views we have at present from the Manor, but as you have brought a plan with you, we will look at it.'

After his lordship and Michael had examined the plan, agreement was reached with one or two alterations. This would mean a pole being put at the rear of the house and an underground cable being laid to supply the electricity to the Manor. The poles crossing the Estate to be positioned along the side of Chaines Wood, and not across fields with crops in. As his lordship remarked, 'this would keep things tidy!'

The same conditions would apply to the Old Gatehouse. As far as the wiring-up of the buildings was concerned, the Electric Company would carry this out and install the lighting and plug points as required throughout the Estate. Mr Jones went on to say that he would be sending his representative to find out what was needed and report back to his lordship for his approval. Should his lordship agree to the company's proposal and costing, the work could be put in hand. When it came to discussing the wiring at the Old Gatehouse, Michael thought it might be wise to have a plug point installed in the lobby, (he was thinking about the tunnel, but didn't say so to anyone present). Once discussions were complete, Mr Jones also mentioned that he was looking into the possibility of putting street lights in the village. Lord Barnes said he thought this would be a very good thing for the safety of the villagers, especially since the escaped prisoner was still at large.

After the two men from the Electricity Company had gone, Lord Barnes asked Mr Parry to make sure that when the men came to put up the poles, they complied with what had been agreed just then at the meeting.

'Make sure,' Lord Barnes said, 'that they do not trample all over the crops in the fields. Also Mr Parry, would you let the tenants in the farm cottages know that they can only have three lighting points and one plug point in each house paid for by the Estate. If they require additional points they must pay for it themselves. Perhaps you could take it upon yourself to be responsible for arranging the order in which the cottages are to be wired up? I know it will be an upset at first, but once the mess is over, I'm sure we will all benefit from it. I will let you know when the representative is coming back, so until then, we can do no more. Now I must inform Mrs Brookes,' said his lordship.

Michael and Lucy returned to their house to give Mrs Craddock the news.

'It will brighten up these dark mornings!' said Mrs Craddock. 'No more filling oil lamps, -that's always a messy job, and not as safe as turning on a light.'

A week later, Mr Jordan from the Electricity Company came to see his lordship.

'I must have my Estates Manager here,' said Lord Barnes.

Following a call from his lordship, Mr Parry joined Lord Barnes and Mr Jordan in the study.

Together they agreed a plan whereby the work would cause as little disturbance as possible. The first thing would be to erect the power line through the Estate, and while this was being done, the wiring-up of the cottages could begin.

'I must tell you, Mr Jordan, there is an escaped prisoner on the loose somewhere around here,' remarked his lordship. 'If you, or anyone in your workforce should come across him, would you raise the alarm?'

'Certainly,' replied Mr Jordan.

'When do you think the workmen will be coming to put the electricity in here?' asked Lord Barnes.

'I will let your lordship know in good time, -it shouldn't be too long now.'

Sorting through his papers, he said, 'I have to go down to the Old Gatehouse next. Thank you for your time!'

'That's my son's house,' remarked Lord Barnes. 'I think you will find him there with his wife.'

Shaking hands with his lordship, Mr Jordan went on his way.

On Friday afternoon, Lord Barnes had a call from Mr Jordan, saying the electrician would be coming to the Manor to start work on the following Monday morning. If this was not convenient, another date could be arranged. Lord Barnes agreed, and straightway sent for Mrs Brookes.

'We will be having the electricians here on Monday morning, Mrs Brookes, but I have a meeting to go to then, so I must leave things in your capable hands.'

'Very good, my lord,' replied Mrs Brookes. 'I will inform the rest of the staff.'

When Florence heard the news, she said to Maud, 'This will mean more clearing up after workmen!'

'Perhaps it won't be too bad,' said Maud.

'I've yet to see workmen do a job without making a mess!' replied Florence.

'Still, it will be better to have a good light to see by,' said Maud.

'-And the dust!' replied Florence, with a laugh.

Monday morning came, and two men appeared at the back door of the kitchen.

'We are from the Electricity Company.'

'Come in,' said Mrs Plum. 'Freda -go and fetch Mrs Brookes. Tell her the electric men are here.'

Freda found Mrs Brookes upstairs talking to Florence and Maud.

'The electric men are here, Mrs Brookes,' said Freda. 'They are in the kitchen.'

'I'm just coming,' replied Mrs Brookes, who then made her way down to the kitchen to attend to them.

'My name is Frank Low and this is Freddie, my mate,' said the electrician.

'I expect you will want to know where to put the lights,' said Mrs Brookes, 'come with me and I will show you.'

When they had gone, Freda said to Mrs Plum, 'Will this take them very long?'

'I don't know,' replied Mrs Plum, with a grin on her face, '-you must ask them!'

She was well aware of what Freda was thinking, she had always got an eye for the young men!

Meanwhile, the work of erecting the poles around the Estate was progressing well. Mr Parry was keeping a sharp eye on what was being done, and was able to report every day to his lordship on the progress being made.

CHAPTER 21

The next day, when Nigel Blair went into the barn to collect a fork, he noticed someone had been sleeping in there. He immediately went to the farm office to call the police, then gathering some of the farm workers together, told them to check all the out-buildings on the farm. As the search was going on, a man ran out from one of the sheds and made off into the nearby woods, hotly pursued by some of the farm workers.

As the man was scrambling through a hedge on the far side of the wood, he fell into one of the holes which had been dug the day before, giving his pursuers a chance to capture him.

News soon reached the Manor that the prisoner had been caught. Thanks to Nigel Blair alerting the police so promptly, the Inspector and Police Sergeant were soon there to take the man away. On hearing the news of the man's capture, there was a general feeling of relief, and the measures which had been put in place to protect people, -especially young women, could now be relaxed. When Florence heard the news, she said she hoped they would put him away for life, '-we can well do without those sort of people being about.'

When Mrs Plum was told, she said, 'Now I won't have to keep going back and forth with Agnes each morning and night, to make sure she arrives safely at the Old Gatehouse.'

Freda thought the walk would do Mrs Plum good and help to get rid of some excess weight, but it was more than her life was worth to say so.

'Maud, I have just had such a shock! -I went into his lordship's bedroom to put a clean towel on his bed, when suddenly, that Freddie popped his head up from the other side of it! He was on the floor pushing wires under the floorboards. Those electricians seem to be everywhere!' exclaimed Florence.

'I shall be glad when they are finished,' said Maud.

'I heard from Freda they will be here for another week, then they have to come back to see everything works,' added

Florence. 'I think they will be working in Mrs Brookes' bedroom tomorrow, so we can keep out of their way!'

The following day was a typical summer's day, with blue skies and sunshine. The electricians arrived as usual, and began work upstairs in the end two bedrooms along the west side landing. After a while there was such a hullaba-loo from Mrs Brookes' bedroom: Freddie had started to remove the bedside rug, but unbeknown to him, it unfor-tunately had a partly charged chamber-pot sitting on it under the bed, the contents of which went everywhere!

A red-faced Freddie ran to find the electrician to tell him what had happened. When Mrs Brookes was told, she hardly said anything. Although a little flustered at first, she soon enlisted the help of a not-so-willing Florence, who ceremoniously carried the rug downstairs to be dealt with.

Frank Low, the electrician, was full of apologies to Mrs Brookes for Freddie's carelessness, saying he should have taken more trouble, and when Florence returned upstairs, she found Maud chortling away to herself.

'It's alright for some people, you didn't have to carry it down,' said Florence, 'oh -it did smell! Mrs Brookes has opened the window in her room to let in some fresh air. I expect we will be told off for not checking all the rooms were made ready for the men to work in. Anyway, I must go downstairs to the library.'

As soon as Florence had gone, Mrs Brookes came into the room where Maud was still chortling to herself.

'I don't know what you have got to laugh about young lady,' said Mrs Brookes. 'Fetch a pail of water and a mop, and follow me.'

Downstairs, the unfortunate Freda had been given the task of immersing the offending rug in a bath of soapy water, and whilst this was a rather unpleasant job, she could still see the funny side of it. Even Frank Low the electrician, though cross with Freddie, was having a job to control himself when anyone spoke about it.

When news of what had happened reached the Old Gatehouse, Mrs Craddock told Lilly it was her job to see the bedrooms were ready each day for the men to begin their work, '-and I must remember to warn Mr Michael and Miss Lucy that they will be having an earlier start than usual next week, when the men arrive.'

Meanwhile, with so much about to be going on in the house, Michael decided to see his father to discuss when a start could be made on exploring the tunnel.

'We must wait until the electricians have finished,' said Lord Barnes.

'I am glad we have decided to ask Mr Parry to help us when we do start finding out what is there. By then, we should be able to take an electric light down the tunnel to see by,' said Michael.

'Yes, we must involve Mr Parry, but I do not want everyone to know what we are doing until we have seen ourselves,' said his lordship. 'I have been reading a book in our library about the time of Charles the Second and Cromwell.'

'That's when the Manor was built!' said Michael.

'That's correct,' replied his lordship, 'and in those days they went to extraordinary lengths to hide supporters of the King. This tunnel of ours might be connected in some way or other with the happenings of that time, -maybe it was used as an escape route?'

'I wonder if that is what Professor Clifton was referring to by his remark regarding 'a small chamber near the mosaic' -he might have been trying to tell us something? This is all very interesting. Well, I think I had better go now and tell Lucy what we have discussed.'

When Michael returned home, Lucy enquired how he had got on.

'We must wait until the electricians have gone before we can explore the tunnel further,' replied Michael. 'When we have the house to ourselves, that will be the time to see what is there.'

'By the way, Michael, a letter came for you. I have put it in your study.'

'Miss Lucy, will there be just Mr Michael and yourself for dinner tonight?' asked Mrs Craddock, entering the room.

'That's right, Mrs Craddock, -just the two of us.'

'Do we know when to expect the electricians here?' asked Mrs Craddock.

'I am not sure,' said Lucy, 'but Michael thinks it might be next week.'

'Thank you, Miss Lucy,' replied Mrs Craddock, returning to the kitchen.

Lucy went to find Michael in his study.

'Lucy, the letter is from my cousin, Robert. He would like to come and spend a few days' holiday with us. When shall I say he can come?'

'Well, not at the moment, Michael. We should wait until the electricians have finished in the house, and then -what about the tunnel?' enquired Lucy, 'Do we want Cousin Robert to know about it? I think you should have a word with your father first before we reply.'

Back at the Manor, Mrs Plum was having words with Mr Jolly, who had come to fix one of the windows in the kitchen. Mrs Plum was busy making a fruitcake, and Mr Jolly was making a mess!

'Must you do that job today?' said a flustered Mrs Plum. 'You workmen never do a job without creating havoc everywhere!'

Freda, who was keeping out of Mrs Plum's way as much as possible, was chuckling away to herself over the ongoing battle of words between two very stubborn combatants, neither wanting to give way to the other. In the end, Freda made an excuse to leave the room so she could have a good laugh. Mr Jolly was secretly enjoying goading Mrs Plum with unflattering remarks about her cooking, which didn't go down well at all!

While Freda was trying to compose herself enough to return to the fray, she was joined by Florence, who was on her way to the kitchen to see Mrs Plum, but on hearing

Freda's account of the ongoing dispute, she said, 'I think I will come back a little later on.'

'That would be wise!' replied Freda, with a broad grin.

On her way back upstairs, she met Mrs Brookes, who said she was going to see Mr Jolly regarding the door on the upstairs cupboard.

'I have just come from there,' said Florence, 'I think Mr Jolly has got his hands full at the moment with Mrs Plum, -if you know what I mean?!'

'Oh!' said Mrs Brookes, taking the hint, 'perhaps it could wait until later on!' She knew what a formidable person Mrs Plum was when ruffled, so thought the cupboard door could wait another day! Instead, she decided to find out how long the electricians were going to be before they finished. Going into the library, she met his lordship coming out with a large book under his arm.

'Do you have any idea how much longer the electricians are going to be?' asked Mrs Brookes.

'I think they will be finished by Friday of this week,' said his lordship. 'Then they will start down at my son's house on Monday. We may have to wait until next week before the lights are switched on though.'

'Thank you, my lord,' replied Mrs Brookes.

CHAPTER 22

On the following Monday, the electricians arrived at the Old Gatehouse to start work.

'It was a good thing Mrs Craddock was here to let them in,' said Mrs Judd, 'because no one was up!'

'I think Miss Lucy and Mr Michael must have over-slept,' said Agnes.

'Quite likely!' replied Mrs Judd. 'It was very misty coming to work this morning, a typical start to a hot summer's day!'

At that moment, Mrs Craddock came into the kitchen.

'Will you start breakfast now, Mrs Judd. Mr Michael and Miss Lucy are about and will be feeling hungry. -Now, I must find Lilly,' said Mrs Craddock, going out of the kitchen and into the hall.

'Ah, there you are Lilly! Will you see to the bedrooms straight away because the electricians will need to start work upstairs first?'

When Lilly went into the main bedroom to tidy up, she nearly fell over Freddie, the electrician's mate, who was on his hands and knees by the bed, carefully rolling up one of the mats.

'I'm sorry, Miss,' said Freddie, hastily.

'Oh, it's my fault,' said Lilly, 'I should have looked where I was going. I just want to tidy up this bed then I will get out of your way.'

On hearing voices in the next room, Frank Low, the electrician, went to see what had happened. He found Freddie still on his hands and knees looking embarrassed, and a flustered maid trying to recover the bedclothes which had fallen over the side of the bed.

'I will soon be out of your way,' said Lilly.

'That's alright, Miss,' replied Frank Low, 'there's no hurry.'

As soon as Lilly had finished, she hurried out of the room and went downstairs to the lobby to tell Agnes all about it.

'We shall just have to get used to having workmen about,' said Agnes, 'but it won't be for long, -a week at the most. That's what I heard Mrs Craddock say.'

Just then, Mrs Judd called out, 'Agnes! Will you bring me some more eggs from the larder?'

'I must go and let you get on,' said Lilly.

Venturing back upstairs to check all the bedrooms were tidy, she found the carpets rolled back, the floorboards up and wires being pulled under the floors. Making a hasty retreat downstairs she met Mrs Craddock.

'I should leave the upstairs until the workmen have finished,' said Mrs Craddock. 'Why not run a duster round the drawing room?'

'If it is empty -alright!' replied Lilly.

Back at the Manor, Lord Barnes had been spending time in the library, reading about conditions in England in the early seventeenth century, in order to try and find out whether there might be a connection between the mosaic at the Old Gatehouse and the tunnel. It was a mystery as to why there was a tunnel there in the first place. The books suggested there may have been buildings on the site of the Old Gatehouse many years earlier, but exactly what, was not clear. Anyway, he intended to find out when the workmen left.

While he was engrossed in his reading, Mrs Brookes went in to tell him that the electric light would be switched on that day.

'Thank you, Mrs Brookes ,' said his lordship, 'I must say it can't come too soon!'

'It will make seeing our way about the house after dark

much safer, my lord, with lights in all the corridors and passages, -especially when the winter comes.'

'I am sure we will all benefit from it, Mrs Brookes.'

Wishing to get on, Lord Barnes turned away and continued looking at the book he was reading.

Later on, Mr Parry came to see his lordship, who was still immersed in his book, in the study. Mr Parry told his lordship that a start was going to be made to get the lights on in the cottages during the day.

'I know,' said his lordship, 'Mrs Brookes told me only an hour ago! By the way, is everything alright about the Estate regarding the work that has just been done? Are you satisfied with how things have gone?'

'Yes, my lord,' said Mr Parry. 'Most of the poles were positioned on the outside of the wood, and only one or two poles can be seen near the houses. Most of the wires have been run underground to the buildings, I think they have tried to comply with your lordship's wishes!'

'Splendid!' replied Lord Barnes.

Just as Mr Parry was leaving, Michael arrived to see his father.

'I thought I would let you know that Lucy and I are going up to town in the morning to choose a light fitting.'

'Alright,' sighed his lordship, sitting back in his chair. 'I am trying to find out something, but so far I have had one interruption after another.'

'I am sorry, father, I didn't mean to disturb you!'

'Oh that's all right, Michael, you were not to know.

Your tunnel is posing quite a problem, -why was it put there? There must have been a reason.'

'Well,' said Michael, 'I will leave you to puzzle it out in peace!'

As Michael was crossing the hall, Mrs Brookes called out to him, 'Michael! Would you ask Lucy if she would come and see me when she has time?'

'I will Mrs Brookes, I shall be seeing her shortly.'

After lunch, the electricians came to switch on the lights at the Manor. Mrs Brookes took them round each room for them to put the bulbs in. Arriving at the study, Mrs Brookes knocked on the door, 'Come in!' called Lord Barnes.

'My lord, I have the electricians here to put the bulbs in.'

'That's good, I shall be able to see what I'm reading!' said his lordship.

When the switch was put on, he exclaimed, 'My word, what a difference that has made! I shall be able to read as much as I like now!'

Thanking the electricians for all their hard work, his lordship said, 'I expect you are much in demand at the moment!'

'That's right, your lordship.'

Mrs Brookes carried on taking the men round to complete fixing the bulbs, finishing in the kitchen with a nice cup of tea.

When Michael and Lucy returned from their shopping expedition, Lucy called at the Manor to see Mrs Brookes.

'You wanted to see me?' said Lucy.

'Yes,' replied Mrs Brookes. 'I thought it wise to have a word with you first. I know it's early - it concerns Christmas cakes and puddings. As you know, Mrs Plum makes a Christmas cake and puddings for the Manor, and when we were talking, she mentioned she was going to make the same for you and Mr. Michael, but I told her I would ask you first, since I didn't want to upset Mrs Judd. We've got plenty of time, she won't be starting Christmas preparations just yet! I think Mrs Plum was trying to be helpful,' said Mrs Brookes.

'Thank you,' replied Lucy, 'how kind! I will have a word with Mrs Judd and let you know, Mrs Brookes.'

On the weekend, Michael said to Lucy, 'Now the workmen have almost finished, can we write to Cousin Robert and invite him to stay?'

'Alright,' replied Lucy, 'it will be nice to see him again. He can have the spare room over the wash-house to sleep in.'

'I will write to him today,' replied Michael, 'then I must go to see Nigel at the farm.'

On the Wednesday morning, the electricians arrived at the Old Gatehouse and knocked on the kitchen door. Mrs Judd asked them in.

'We have come to switch the lights on,' said Frank Low.

'If you wait here,' said Mrs Judd, 'I will see if I can find Mrs Craddock.'

When she arrived, Frank Low said, 'We would like to start upstairs first.'

'Very good,' replied Mrs Craddock.

Taking a pair of steps and a box of bulbs, the two men made their way upstairs to the bedrooms. Then they worked their way downstairs, ending up in the kitchen. Mrs Judd, being an inquisitive sort, asked Frank Low when he thought he would be going to finish at her cottage.

While they were engaged in conversation, Freddie, who had tried to get to know Agnes when he was working there earlier, saw his chance, and picking up the box of bulbs and steps, went out into the wash-house hoping to chat-up Agnes, but she was having none of it! She turned her back on him, and got on with her job, folding clothes at the wash-house table. Freddie, feeling put out by this, took one of the bulbs and, climbing up on the steps, reached out to put it in the lampholder. In so doing, the bulb slipped out of his fingers. Making a desperate attempt to grab hold of it as it made it's way to the stone floor, he overbalanced, falling off the steps. At the same time, the bulb landed just behind Agnes and exploded with a resounding bang! Agnes screamed and fled into the kitchen.

'Oh my gawd, what was that?' said Mrs Judd, dropping the plate she was holding. Mrs Craddock, who had happened to be in the next room, came hurrying in to see what the commotion was. Seeing Agnes in tears, and Mrs Judd picking up the pieces of plate from the floor, she said, 'What has been going on, Mrs Judd?'

Just then, Frank Low, -who had gone to rescue Freddie from amongst the steps, came into the kitchen with the young lad, who was limping and nursing a rather nasty cut on his leg.

'Are you alright young man?' asked Mrs Craddock.

'I think so,' replied Freddie.

'That leg wants a bandage round it,' said Mrs Craddock. 'I'll see to it.'

Agnes, who by now had recovered from her fright, was sweeping up the glass from the floor of the wash-house.

'Whatever was that noise?' asked Lilly, who had been tidying upstairs, 'it sounded like a shot!'

'It's alright,' said Frank. 'My mate dropped a bulb and it made a bang!'

'Have you much more to do?' enquired Mrs Craddock, drily.

'We have just about finished. I think there's only the wood-shed to do, then we will leave you in peace!'

'Thank you,' replied a relieved Mrs Craddock.

CHAPTER 23

When Michael arrived at the farm, he found Phillis Blair holding on to one of the horses while her father was examining it's legs.

'What's wrong with him?' asked Michael.

'I think he's hurt his leg, he's not walking right,' said Nigel, 'but I can't see any cause for it at the moment. Phillis, will you walk him round again so I can have another look?'

They both stood and watched, then Michael said, 'Has he got something in his hoof?'

'I couldn't see anything,' replied Nigel, 'but I'd better have another look.'

Lifting the horse's leg up again, Nigel Blair started to scrape away at the underside of the hoof and immediately the horse withdrew it as if it hurt.

'I think you have found the trouble,' said Michael. 'Do you think I could have a look in the dairy with you sometime soon, now that we have mains electricity on? Would you be free this afternoon, Nigel?'

'I would,' replied the farm manager, 'shall I see you there?'

'Yes,' said Michael.

Leaving the farm, Michael returned home to find Lucy.

'By the way, Lucy, there is a Summer Fair being held in Drybridge at the moment. Would you like to go tomorrow?'

'Rather!' exclaimed Lucy, 'that would make a real change. I've not been to a fair for some time. One year, my mother and father took me and my Dad won a coconut! That was such fun! Also, it will give Mrs Judd a rest from me being around!'

The next morning, after breakfast, Michael and Lucy set off to spend the day at the Fair.

When they arrived, Michael said, 'I will try to win you a coconut!'

It took him several attempts, but in the end Michael was lucky. Lucy was delighted!

The stalls and fair rides were all lit up with coloured lights.

'Look!' said Lucy, 'there's a stall with rock. - I must

157

have some. When I was young I used to like the pinky-red pieces, they tasted of cloves.'

Going over to the stall, Michael said, 'I can remember my father buying some rock when we were on holiday abroad - it was Carnival week where we were staying. I was surprised at him liking it! There were stalls all around the market-place, and I can remember there was a carousel there as well!'

'It is surprising,' said Lucy, with a chuckle. 'I would never have thought your father would like rock, but there, you can't tell, can you? Shall we take some back for him as a joke?' said Lucy, 'or do you think he would be offended?'

'No,' replied Michael, 'I think it will make him smile to think that I had remembered he liked it.'

Lucy bought two bags of rock from the stall, and putting them in her basket, she remarked, 'I must be with you when you give your father the rock, so I can see his face. I do hope he will like it!'

After they had had a good look round, Michael and Lucy left the Fair and made their way back to the Old Gatehouse.

The next day, Michael and Lucy went up to the Manor. Mrs Brookes said his lordship was in the study, and after telling her of their day out, they made their way to find him.

'We have brought you something, father,' said Michael, with a smile on his face.

Taking the paper bag, with a certain amount of

caution, his lordship looked inside. A broad grin appeared on his face, '-You remembered, Michael!'

'Yes, father! I told Lucy all about our holiday and the stalls around the market-place, and as you like rock, we thought we would bring you some.'

Taking a piece of rock out of the bag, Lord Barnes thanked them and popped it into his mouth, -much to the amusement of Lucy, who was seeing a side of her father-in-law she had not witnessed before! Feeling happy with the outcome of their visit, Michael and Lucy left his lordship to enjoy his rock.

When they arrived home, Mrs Craddock said she had put the post on the table in the study.

'Thank you,' replied Michael.

Going into the study, he picked up the letters, and sorting through them said, 'Look, Lucy, there is a letter here from Robert.'

After reading it, Michael said, 'He would like to come and stay on Friday.'

'That's the day after tomorrow!' exclaimed Lucy. 'Well, that's alright as far as accommodation is concerned. He can have the bedroom over the wash-house.'

'It will be nice to see him again,' said Michael. 'We always manage to find something to chat about when we meet!'

'I must tell Mrs Craddock that Robert will be here on Friday, she will make sure his room is ready.'

'I think my father mentioned he was expecting company today,' said Michael. 'Lord and Lady Finsbour are coming for a few days. I hope my father does not expect us to entertain them, -in any case, we shall have Robert here.'

Up at the Manor, preparations were being made to welcome Lord and Lady Finsbour.

'I am glad it's not that old Colonel and Mrs Parks,' said Florence.

'So am I!' replied Maud.

'I wonder if her ladyship wears a night cap? You had better be careful, Maud, if she does,' said Florence, with a laugh, 'or you might be accused of pinching it!'

'Florence! Is everything ready up here?' asked Mrs Brookes.

'Yes,' replied Florence, 'we have finished the bedrooms. They have all been cleaned and the beds made.'

'Will you both go down to see if the library wants anything doing to it, then check the drawing room?'

'Right, Mrs Brookes!' replied Florence.

Down in the kitchen, Mrs Plum was wrestling with a large chicken which she was preparing for dinner that evening.

'Freda! Will you bring me the biggest onion you can find? I need it for the chicken.'

After a short while, Freda came into the kitchen, holding two large onions in her hands. Mrs Plum took one of the onions, peeled it, then stuffed it into the chicken, exclaiming as she did so, 'there's nothing like an onion to give the chicken a good flavour!'

Covering it with a cloth, she put it to one side while she got on with preparing the vegetables.

Mrs Brookes had been waiting for the visitors to arrive and caught sight of the carriage coming up the drive towards the Manor. Making her way across the hall to the front door, she called out to Florence, who had just left the library, to let his lordship know the guests had arrived. As she waited at the entrance to the Manor, she was joined by Lord Barnes, who welcomed Lord and Lady Finsbour to Caiston Manor. Lord Barnes and Lord Finsbour were old friends, and often communicated with each other on business matters, relating to the running of their estates.

'I have told my driver to return home, and to come back to collect my wife and self in three days' time,' said Lord Finsbour. 'I would have liked to have stopped longer, but I have to chair a meeting of our local farmers' association then. It is a busy time of year just now.'

Then Lord Barnes began to tell his friend about the happenings that had taken place since the wedding, and how one of his staff had been attacked by an escaped prisoner.

'I had better go and find my wife then!' chuckled Lord Finsbour.

'I should think Mrs Brookes is looking after her in the drawing room,' replied Lord Barnes, 'I'll finish telling you all about it later!'

CHAPTER 24

The next day, at breakfast, Michael said to Lucy, 'Robert should be here today. I do hope the weather stays nice for him while he's here.'

And so, just before lunch, a carriage arrived at the Old Gatehouse and Robert stepped out.

'It's good to see you again!' said Michael. 'This is my wife, Lucy. What was your journey like?'

'A bit eventful!' replied Robert, 'I will be glad to get out of these things!'

'Let me show you to your room,' said Lucy, 'then come down and join us for some lunch.'

After a short while, Robert joined Michael and Lucy in the dining room.

'I hope you are hungry,' said Lucy.

'I'm famished!' replied Robert.

'He was always hungry when I knew him!' laughed Michael. 'I hope the weather stays like this while you're here, so I can show you around with everything looking at it's best!'

'I will introduce you to our housekeeper, Mrs Craddock,' said Lucy.

'-Be careful not to cross her, Robert, or it will be the worse for you!' advised Michael, jokingly.

'Oh, she is not as bad as that,' said Lucy, 'he is pulling your leg, Robert!'

Michael and Robert spent the afternoon chatting about old times (which Lucy found very entertaining), and also about the mosaic at the bottom of their garden.

Robert asked, 'Does the lake ever freeze over in the winter months?'

'It did last winter,' replied Michael, 'but it didn't last very long.'

'Why did you ask?' enquired Lucy, 'do you ice-skate, Robert?'

'Yes,' replied Robert. 'I do, whenever I get the chance.'

'It's got to get very cold for the lake to freeze, -how long were you thinking of staying, Robert?' laughed Michael.

'Till next Thursday if that's convenient?' replied Robert.

'Yes, quite convenient,' smiled Lucy.

At breakfast the next morning, Robert asked, 'How ever does Michael manage with the house full of women? This could drive a man silly!'

'Oh, you need not worry, I keep a sharp eye on him when they are around!' said Lucy. 'We have only got a small staff here at present, not like all those up at the Manor!'

'Perhaps, Michael, we ought to call on your father?' replied Robert, with a smile.

'Yes,' said Michael. 'I thought we would pay him a short visit today, -he will be pleased to see you again.'

When they had left for the Manor, Mrs Craddock said to Lucy, 'That Mr Robert is a character! I heard him and Mr Michael having a laugh about something, they seem to get along together very well.'

'Yes, they do,' said Lucy. 'They are old friends.'

'Mrs Brookes will have her hands full if Mr Robert spends much time up at the Manor, -if you know what I mean!' went on Mrs Craddock, with a chuckle.

'I don't think she needs to worry too much!' said Lucy, hopefully.

Michael and Robert arrived at the Manor and went straight to the study to see Lord Barnes.

'I've brought Cousin Robert to see you father. He is staying with us at the house until Thursday.'

'Good to see you, Robert,' said Lord Barnes, extending a hand to his nephew. 'How are you?'

'Very well thank you, my lord.'

'I'm glad you brought some nice weather with you!' said Lord Barnes. 'They say it's going to stay like this for the next week. You must show Robert round while he's here, Michael.'

'I was going to father, but I thought I would bring him to see you first.'

'Well, it's nice to see you again, Robert, but don't let me delay you now. If you should happen to see Mrs Brookes on your way out, Michael, would you ask her to come and see me?'

'I will, father,' said Michael.

On leaving the study, Michael said to Robert, 'I think Mrs Brookes might be in the kitchen at this time of day.'

Making their way down, they found Mrs Brookes, Mrs Plum, Freda, Florence and Maud chattering away over a cup of tea. When Michael and Robert walked in, Michael said, 'It seems we've come at the right time, Robert!'

'Would you like a cup of tea?' asked Mrs Plum.

Before Michael could decline Mrs Plum's kind offer, Robert said, 'Yes please!' looking round the room as he said it.

While Mrs Plum was attending to the tea, Michael said, 'Mrs Brookes, we have just left my father in the study and he asked if you would go to see him?'

'Yes, I will,' said Mrs Brookes, and putting down her cup and saucer, she left the room.

'I think I ought to make a move too,' said Florence.

'Now see what you have done, Michael,' said Robert, winking at Florence. 'Everyone is going, -just as I was beginning to enjoy myself!'

'Well, let's finish our tea, then we must be on our way,' replied Michael.

After they had gone, Mrs Plum said to Freda, 'That one wants watching or there will be trouble for someone. He's got an eye for the young ladies.'

'He's not my sort!' said Freda, 'I hope he doesn't come bothering me, I've got a young man already.'

'I was thinking about Agnes and Lilly at the Old Gatehouse,' replied Mrs Plum, 'because that is where he's staying. Still, I think Miss Lucy will have got the measure of him by now and she will keep an eye open for any hanky-panky, I'm sure.'

'I hope Mr Michael takes him about the Estate where he can't get into mischief with anyone,' said Freda.

'Do not be too sure!' replied Mrs Plum. 'I shall be relieved when I hear he has gone away!'

Michael and Robert left the Manor and made their way to the farm to see Nigel Blair. While they were there, Phillis Blair returned from a ride. Seeing Michael and Robert, she thought she would find out who the dark-haired young man was. Robert wanted nothing better than to chat to this very desirable young lady, to the exclusion of Michael and Nigel, who were busy discussing how the injured horse was progressing. When Michael had finished talking to Nigel, he looked round for Robert, who was nowhere to be seen! Since Phillis Blair had also disappeared, Michael made his way to where she stabled her horse, only to find Phillis and Robert in a passionate embrace on a heap of straw in the barn. Withdrawing from the scene, Michael walked a few paces away, then called out, 'Robert!'

After a few minutes, Robert appeared, a little flushed, but in a very buoyant mood.

'We should be getting back now,' said Michael, crossly. 'Lucy will be wondering where we have got to.'

That night, when Michael and Lucy were in bed, Michael related to Lucy what had happened on the visit to the farm.

'We mustn't leave him alone without one of us being present,' said Lucy.

'I thought I knew Robert,' said Michael, 'but he's changed. We still get on well, but he likes the ladies too much! He's got a roving eye!'

'Oh goodness! -We've got him here until Thursday!' sighed Lucy.

After breakfast the next morning, Lord Barnes sent a message asking for Michael to go up to the Manor to see him. Robert said he would go for a walk down to the lake while Michael was gone.

'I don't think it is cold enough for skating,' teased Lucy, '-but the fresh air will do you good!'

On his way back, Robert thought he would come round by the woodshed and into the wash-house by the back door, giving him a chance to chat up Agnes, in case she was doing some washing there. But Mrs Judd had been on the lookout for Robert, and seeing him approaching, called Agnes into the kitchen on the pretext of wanting help. When Robert entered the wash-house he found it empty, so he walked through into the kitchen.

Robert said to Mrs Judd, 'Do you know what time Michael will be back? Did he say how long he would be?'

'I'm sure I don't know,' replied Mrs Judd. 'All I know is, Mr Michael has gone to see his father.'

'I think I will have a walk up to the Manor to meet Michael,' said Robert, 'it's a nice, sunny day outside.'

Leaving the kitchen, Robert made his way out of the house and on to the drive which led up to the Manor.

Michael and Lord Barnes had been making plans for the exploration of the tunnel in Michael's garden. They needed Mr Parry's help to open the small door in the wall, and decided it would be wise to make a hole in the roof at the far end of the tunnel where the small door was, providing easier access and more air. Until it was known what was there, they would need to proceed with caution. Lord Barnes said he would get Mr Parry to make a start once their respective guests had left, and if asked what he was doing, to say it was to do with the drains.

Just as Michael was leaving his father, Robert turned up at the Manor. 'I thought I would come to meet you,' said Robert, 'it's such a nice day. Shall we go riding?'

'Alright!' replied Michael.

For the next three days, Michael and Robert spent most of the time together, riding about the Estate.

Then the morning came for Robert to leave.

'It has been good to see you again,' said Michael.

'Thank you for having me!' replied Robert, 'I think you are very fortunate, Michael, to have such a lovely wife as Lucy. You're a lucky man.'

CHAPTER 25

The next day, as Michael and Lucy were just finishing breakfast, there came a knock on the dining room door.

'I'm sorry to disturb you,' said Mrs Craddock, 'but Mr Parry is here and wants to know if it is alright for him to carry on down the garden.'

'Yes, of course, Mrs Craddock,' replied Michael, with a smile. Turning back to Lucy, he said, 'Mr Parry has come to see to the drains. It may take him a little while.'

When Mrs Craddock had gone, Lucy started to laugh and said, 'I don't know of any drains at the bottom of the garden, my father would surely have told me when he put the fruit trees in!'

'Actually, Mr Parry is going to dig down and break through into the tunnel, to try to find out what is under the mosaic floor,' said Michael, 'I just didn't want to say that in front of Mrs Craddock! It's as well we keep things quiet at this stage.'

'I will ask Mrs Craddock to see Mr Parry has a refreshing drink while he is here, then,' said Lucy, 'it will be thirsty work!'

'-And I ought to have a word with him before I go up to the Manor to see father,' said Michael.

Leaving Lucy in the drawing room, Michael went on his way.

Later on in the day, Mr Parry went to see his lordship to update him on his progress.

'I have cleared a place in front of the door in question, and it only needs breaking open now. I don't think we should wait too long before we do that, in case the weather changes. It's perfect right now.'

'Very well,' replied his lordship, 'how about tomorrow morning? Shall we say ten o'clock?'

'That'll suit me fine,' replied Mr Parry.

'I will have a word with my son to let him know,' said Lord Barnes.

Next morning, after breakfast, Michael and Lucy got ready to receive Lord Barnes. Lucy had asked Mrs Craddock to serve refreshments later, on their return to the house. Just before ten o'clock his lordship appeared. Mr Parry had arrived earlier and had everything prepared ready. Mrs Craddock ushered Lord Barnes inside whilst Michael and Lucy put on their shoes.

'Right!' said Lord Barnes. 'Shall we go and see what's there?'

As the three made their way down the garden path, Mrs Judd, who had been watching proceedings from the kitchen window, said, 'I shouldn't have thought his lordship would come here just to look at drains! There's more going on here than we've been told!'

On arrival at the bottom of the garden, they found Mr Parry waiting, and after exchanging a few words of greeting, he climbed down the ladder to the iron door.

'I shall have to break the hinges in order to get the door open,' he called out. 'They are all rusted up, so that should not be too much of a problem.'

After a few blows with his hammer, the door partly opened.

'I think it is held from the inside,' exclaimed Mr Parry. '-Uggghhh! - the smell down here is awful!'

Using a crowbar, he gave the door one final wrench, and as he did so, it fell off.

'Phew!' said Mr Parry, covering his face with his cap as he coughed and gasped for breath.

'Get him out, get him out!' cried Lord Barnes.

Michael ran towards the ladder to help Mr Parry out, whilst his lordship and Lucy stood back. Climbing up the ladder, and emerging into fresh air, Mr Parry said, 'The stench down there is vile - it quite took my breath away. I have never smelt such an obnoxious odour in all my life!'

Still holding a handkerchief over her face, Lucy said, 'Let's get away from this awful smell and go back to the house for a moment - perhaps the air will clear a bit!'

'I think that would be very wise,' said his lordship.

After a cup of tea and a biscuit, Lord Barnes asked Mr Parry how he was feeling and if he was up to carrying out further investigation. Mr Parry said, 'I'm ready to have another go. I'm as anxious as you, my lord, to see what's there!'

They all made their way outside again.

Climbing down the ladder, Mr Parry asked, 'Would you pass the lantern down to me?'

Standing in front of the open doorway, he held the lantern inside and looked in. Reeling back, as if he had seen a ghost, and with a look of terror on his face, he fell back on to the ladder. Michael reached down and seized hold of Mr Parry, who was as white as a sheet and shaking.

'Let's get him out!' cried Lord Barnes.

Slowly, Mr Parry made his way up the ladder with help from Michael. Turning to Lord Barnes, Mr Parry said, in a hoarse voice, 'There are two bodies in the small chamber, -the smell is terrible, -they are just skeletons with clothes on!'

'Oh, my dear fellow, we must get you inside. Michael, take him indoors and get him a brandy, he has had a shock. Say nothing to the staff until we can sort out what to do.'

'Right, father,' said Michael, 'let's get Mr Parry into the house, Lucy.'

For a few minutes, Lord Barnes stood looking at the hole, then he followed the three of them inside.

'How are you now?' asked Lord Barnes.

'I feel much better already, my lord,' replied Mr Parry, draining his glass of brandy. 'I suppose I should have been more prepared, looking into an unknown place like that. I am quite ready to investigate again, now I know what to expect.'

'Well, only if you feel up to it!' said his lordship. 'You have had quite a shock!'

Making their way back down the garden path, the trio looked on whilst Mr Parry climbed down the ladder, taking the lantern with him. After looking inside the room with his handkerchief over his nose, he returned to the ladder.

'The two bodies have each got a sort of leather pouch slung around them. Their clothing has perished and will quite possibly fall off when touched. They both have swords. There is also a table, and one of the bodies seems to have been in a sitting position. The other is on the floor.'

'Thank you,' said Lord Barnes. 'Let's get you out, I am sorry you have had to see such a gruesome sight. I think it best if we put the cover back in case it rains tonight, then I must have a word with the Police Inspector. Let's all go back to the house now.'

'I bet tongues are doing overtime in the kitchen!' remarked Michael, 'Mrs Judd will be imagining all sorts of things for Mr Parry to have looked like he did!'

'Well, it will make a change from the tittle-tattle about poor old Mrs Franklyn in the village,' replied Lucy, with a smile.

When they entered the house, Mrs Craddock took one look at Mr Parry's ashen face and immediately asked, 'Are you alright? Whatever has happened now?'

'Yes, thank you, Mrs Craddock, I just had a bit of a shock, -that's all!' he replied.

'Perhaps you would ask Mrs Judd to make us a cup of tea please, Mrs Craddock? We'll be in Michael's study,' said Lucy.

There was much to discuss, but first of all, Lord Barnes contacted the Police Inspector, who said he would be on his way immediately and not to touch anything.

'Just time for our cup of tea!' said Lord Barnes, as Mrs Craddock appeared with the tea tray.

Suitably refreshed, they made their way to the hole at the end of the tunnel, where they were soon joined by the Inspector. Once Mr Parry had related his experience and what he had seen, the Inspector took a quick look into the chamber, and climbing quickly back up the ladder said, 'Leave it with me. I will have to contact the appropriate authorities, but meantime, put the cover back over the hole. Let nothing be disturbed and keep everybody away.'

When the Inspector had taken his leave, Lord Barnes remarked that he had hoped to keep the discovery of the tunnel quiet, -he certainly hadn't expected to find human remains there.

'Once this gets out, there will be rumours all over the village! We must be prepared, Michael, for onlookers and even trespassers, who will want to see for themselves what's going on. If reporters come, send them up to me. I will give them as little information as possible, but you will need to brief your staff of our findings and ask them to be both vigilant and discreet. I must do the same at the Manor.'

At that, Mr Parry said, 'Well, my lord, I'll be on my way now. I feel perfectly recovered. What a day it's been!'

'I can't thank you enough for all your help in this. We certainly couldn't have managed without you!' said Lord Barnes, shaking Mr Parry warmly by the hand.

On his arrival back, Mrs Brookes went into the study to see his lordship.

'I thought I would have a word to find out if Mr Parry is alright after his ordeal? I have been speaking to Mrs Craddock who mentioned something had happened.'

'Yes, thank you, Mrs Brookes, it is kind of you to ask. I think I need to explain what has occurred.'

He proceeded to tell Mrs Brookes of the day's happenings and to ask for her help in keeping the staff informed.

'It was a horrible sight for Mr Parry to witness -none of us expected to find human remains there. We have got to wait until the Inspector tells us what is to be done next, so please advise everyone to say nothing in the village.'

'Thank you, my lord, I will, and I will also let the staff know Mr Parry is alright - they were concerned. Mr Parry has a good many friends here, and we all think a lot of him.'

'That is nice to know,' replied his lordship. 'I too, hold Mr Parry in the greatest esteem.'

Meanwhile, back at the Old Gatehouse, Lucy was relaying to Michael how Mrs Judd had been complaining about a nasty smell in her kitchen.

'Oh, I think I know what that is!' replied Michael. 'It will be coming along the tunnel into the lobby, and seeping around the trapdoor Mr Parry put in. I will go and see her.'

Michael went into the kitchen and said to Mrs Judd, 'That smell will soon go away. Now we have discovered where it is coming from, it can be dealt with.'

'Oh, that's good!' said Mrs Judd, 'it's not as bad as when Mr Parry came in earlier though. -Why was his lordship here?'

'As I said, we found something nasty down the garden, Mrs Judd, and as soon as we can get rid of it, the smell should go away. I will be speaking to all the staff very shortly to explain what has been discovered here today, and can tell you more then.'

'Is Mr Parry alright now?'

'-Yes, Mrs Judd, quite well thank you. I will let you get on with your work,' replied Michael, going back to the drawing room to find Lucy.

'Mrs Judd is an inquisitive old so-and-so isn't she?' said Michael.

'She is!' replied Lucy. 'She likes to know all that is going on in the house.'

CHAPTER 26

Michael arrived at the Manor to see his father. Finding his lordship in the study, Michael asked him if he had heard anything more from the Inspector.

'No,' said Lord Barnes, 'but I think I will get in touch with Professor Clifton and acquaint him with what we have found. Perhaps he would come and see for himself, and be able to give us an explanation as to why those two men were in that room and who they were?'

'It will be good if Professor Clifton could come,' said Michael, 'you told me he was a great authority on

antiquities. Can you get in touch with him today, father?'
'I will try,' replied Lord Barnes.

Suddenly, there was a knock on the door.

'Come in!' said Lord Barnes.

The door opened and in walked the Inspector.

'I hope I'm not interrupting anything, my lord?'

'No,' replied Lord Barnes, 'I was just telling my son that I will be getting in touch with Professor Clifton regarding the discoveries we have made, -are you happy with this?'

'That's what I have come to see you about,' said the Inspector. 'The powers-that-be have decided to put everything on hold for the moment, until an expert can be found to give an opinion on what is there. If you can arrange for the Professor to come, he is such an eminent man that his input would be invaluable, but keep me informed, this is still a police matter. I will need to speak to him myself.'

Just as Michael was leaving the study, he heard a commotion at the front door. Going to see what it was all about, he saw Mrs Brookes, surrounded by reporters all clamouring to ask her questions. Michael quickly returned to the study and told the Inspector what was going on outside.

'Come with me,' said the Inspector to Michael. 'Let's go and sort this out!'

When they reached the front door, the Inspector ordered the reporters to leave, or risk being summonsed for trespassing on private land.

'Oh, I am so glad to see you!' said Mrs Brookes. 'They just would not go away!'

'That's alright,' said the Inspector, '-if you have any more trouble, just let me know and I will deal with it.'

'I hope they don't go down to the house,' said Michael.

'I think I will put a man on duty there, just in case,' said the Inspector.

'Thank you,' replied Michael.

When he arrived home, he found a few reporters standing outside his house. As soon as they caught sight of Michael, they started asking all sorts of questions, but at that moment, a policeman appeared and told them to move on.

'Thank you,' said Michael.

'That's alright, sir,' replied the policeman. 'I shall be about here for a while, so you have no need to worry.'

Michael thought he would go in by the kitchen door, but when he opened it, he nearly got attacked by an irate Mrs Judd, wielding a mop!

'Oh! I'm so sorry, Mr Michael, I thought it was another one of those reporters come to bother us. They tried to get Agnes to say what had happened this morning, when she was on her way to work, but she managed to get away from them.'

'Don't worry, we should be alright now,' said Michael. 'There is a policeman standing outside to keep the reporters away.'

'Thank goodness!' replied Mrs Judd.

'I must go and find my wife,' said Michael.

Leaving the kitchen, he went into the drawing room to find Lucy.

'Where's that lovely wife of mine?' said Michael, taking Lucy in his arms and giving her a loving kiss.

'Michael!' exclaimed Lucy. 'Someone may come in!'

'Well, that's alright!' replied Michael, giving her another one! 'We live here!'

'Tell me what your father had to say,' said Lucy, moving away from Michael.

'My father is going to contact Professor Clifton to see if he would come and advise us on what we have found,' replied Michael. 'The Inspector welcomed his involvement in this.'

'Poor Mr Parry! It must have been a very great shock for him when he looked inside the room and saw those two bodies!' said Lucy.

'It was,' replied Michael. 'He went as white as a sheet. I'm afraid he will remember it for a very long time!'

'-Changing the subject, has your father said any more about when we are to expect delivery of the boat, Michael?'

'It should be here some time in the New Year. Then I will take you sailing on the lake. It's not really large, more of a dinghy, and just big enough for us two!'

'I shall look forward to that,' replied Lucy. 'How exciting!'

Just then, the telephone rang in the study.

'I had better go and answer that,' said Michael, leaving Lucy in the drawing room.

Michael picked up the phone.

'Is that you, Michael?'

'Yes, father!'

'I have just heard from Professor Clifton and he will be here tomorrow morning, to see what we have uncovered. I must also let the Inspector know,' said his lordship. 'I hope we have a fine day for it.'

'So do I,' replied Michael.

CHAPTER 27

After breakfast, the next morning, a large black vehicle drew up outside the Old Gatehouse and four men, dressed in white overalls, got out. Then followed a police car with the Inspector and two constables. Shortly afterwards, Mr Parry and his lordship arrived. Mr Parry went straight down the garden to uncover the hole, ready for inspection, whilst Mrs Craddock invited Lord Barnes in, showing him into the drawing room, where he was soon joined by Michael and Lucy.

'Now, we just need the Professor to arrive, then we can get on,' said Lord Barnes.

They didn't have to wait long, and after introductions had been made, Lord Barnes asked Michael to lead the way, and off they all went, down to the mosaic where Mr Parry was waiting. Professor Clifton said he would like to look inside the room before anything was disturbed. Climbing down the ladder, lantern in hand, the Professor peered inside the room. After a few moments, he stood back from the doorway, exclaiming, 'Remarkable! I have never seen anything like this before. I think we must make a detailed record of this before anything is touched.'

Climbing back up the ladder, the Professor instructed one of the four men to take photographs of the inside of the room and it's contents - if that should prove possible. Whilst another, should make a detailed sketch of how things were found inside the chamber, and then itemise everything. When all that had been done, the Inspector gave instructions for the two bodies to be removed.

Not wanting to witness this, Lucy said she would return to the house, and hurried quickly away on hearing Lord Barnes ask if the two bodies would be taken to the local mortuary. His lordship said that if the men were eventually buried in the local church cemetery, on the boundary of the Estate, he would pay all expenses.

'That seems to be a good way of dealing with this case,' said the Inspector. 'As for the items these unfortunate men had on their person, a court of enquiry must decide ownership. My men will be present when the clothes and possessions are being removed from the bodies. These will be held at the Police Station until after the court of enquiry has determined what has to be done.'

'That is agreed then,' said Lord Barnes to the Inspector. 'I shall also be interested in what Professor Clifton makes of all this!'

After everything had been taken from the chamber, Mr Parry put the cover back over the hole.

'Now we shall have to decide what to do with the room,' said Lord Barnes. 'We will have to give it some careful thought, Michael.'

'Yes, we will, father. Shall we return to the house with the Professor, now he has seen things moved safely into the police vehicle?'

'Let us ask him,' said Lord Barnes.

'I would rather like to follow things through, and to supervise the safe removal of the effects,' remarked the Professor. 'Then I should be glad to have a word with you.'

'Certainly,' replied Lord Barnes. 'Please join me at the Manor when you are ready.'

The Professor left and Michael said to his father, 'Let's go and find Lucy in the house.'

As they made their way back, they were joined by Mr Parry, and all three went inside to enjoy some liquid refreshment.

'Come and sit down,' said Lucy. 'You must be tired from standing out there. I had to come in when I knew the bodies were going to be brought out! -To think they had been lying there all that time, and us not knowing anything about it!'

'Thank you again for your help in all this,' said Lord Barnes to Mr Parry. 'I don't know what we would have done without your assistance.'

'It has been an interesting exercise - even though it was a bit of a shock, seeing those two bodies! I'm curious to know exactly how long they have been in there,' remarked Mr Parry.

'I am hoping the Professor will be able to tell us more when he returns. I think those two leather bags contained coins, and that was why he wanted to see them safely in the hands of the Inspector,' replied his lordship. 'I don't know how long the Professor will be, but I said I would see him back at the Manor, so I had better be on my way.'

'Do we know what will happen to the room down there?' Mr Parry asked Michael.

'This is something we must talk about when we see the Professor,' replied Michael.

'I wonder what my father will say when he sees the garden?' said Lucy. 'He spent a lot of time getting it round and now look at it!'

'I have left everything covered up down there until we know what is to be done!' said Mr Parry. 'I think it's time I was on my way. Let me know if you need help with anything else.'

'Thank you once again, Mr Parry,' said Michael.

That afternoon, the Professor called to see Lord Barnes to discuss the morning's happenings. He said he would need to make further enquiries regarding the tunnel, the room and it's contents, since he was sure there was more to be found out as to why these things were there. He would then be in a better position to say what it was all about.

When the Professor had gone, Lord Barnes got in touch with Michael and told him what the Professor had said.

'Well,' said Michael, 'it will give us more time with Christmas just around the corner. Incidentally, I think Lucy's on her way to see Mrs Brookes about Christmas right now, -there's a lot to think about!'

Lucy found Mrs Brookes in the kitchen, talking to Mrs Plum.

'I don't like the way the evenings are beginning to close in,' said Lucy.

'The mornings too!' added Freda. 'I will soon be coming to work in the dark!'

'We shall have to start thinking about Christmas cakes and puddings,' said Mrs Plum.

'One word about Christmas in our house,' said Freda, 'and my two young brothers go wild with excitement!'

'Oh, it's a lovely time of year,' replied Lucy. 'Coming back home from church on Christmas morning, with the ground covered with snow, and everyone wishing each other a Happy Christmas, then to walk into a warm room with a fire blazing away, and the smell from the kitchen of the goose being cooked, -it's then you feel all of a glow and happy to be alive!'

'My sentiments entirely!' replied Mrs Brookes, 'you could not have put it better, Lucy! This will be the first Christmas in your new home. With the two extra bedrooms, you should manage alright when the time comes for you to entertain guests.'

'Yes, although I thought the new bedrooms would be suitable for our live-in staff,' said Lucy. 'Now, what exactly did you want to ask me, Mrs Brookes?'

The two of them made their way to Mrs Brookes' room.

'Have you given any thought to Christmas arrangements, Miss Lucy?'

'I hope to have a word with my husband later today, then I will let you know. By the way, I had a word with Mrs Judd about our Christmas cake, and she wants to make it for us. I hope Mrs Plum will understand.'

When Lucy arrived home, it was evident things were not quite right in the kitchen from the commotion going on. As she approached the doorway, she heard a distraught Mrs Judd being consoled by Mrs Craddock. There was a smell of burning. Making a hasty retreat, Lucy made her way to the study.

'I think Mrs Judd has burnt our Christmas cake! I don't think she's got the hang of that cooking range yet. I must go and see she's all right, -but I'll give it a few moments first!'

'Hmm, I think it best if I stay here in my study until things calm down a bit!' said Michael, not wishing to become involved in domestic mishaps.

After a little while, Lucy managed to persuade Mrs Judd to try again, adding that her mother had warned that cooking ranges were notorious for burning things, and that Mrs Judd's cake was not the first or the last to get rather well done! It was just a matter of gauging the oven temperature. Agnes, who had made herself scarce in the wash-house during this time, appeared in the kitchen.

'There you are!' said Mrs Judd, pulling herself together, 'you can get rid of that burnt offering in the rubbish bin, and then come and help me get the things together ready to make another one tomorrow morning, -it won't take us long.'

'How is 'Cook'?' asked Michael later, with a grin on his face.

'Oh, she's all right now,' replied Lucy. 'It's very disheartening when something like that happens. I'm sure Mrs Judd wants things to be right for us. Anyway, she and Agnes are going to try again tomorrow!'

'Let's hope all goes well!' said Michael.

CHAPTER 28

'Michael,' said Lucy. 'Did your father mention anything about Christmas when you were speaking yesterday?'

'No,' said Michael. 'What are you thinking we should do?'

'Well,' said Lucy, 'this will be my first Christmas away from home, and I know it's the first Christmas of our married life, but I was wondering what your father will be doing on Christmas Day -apart from us all meeting up at church? I have been giving this some thought. -Now this is only just a suggestion, but if we both joined your father after church on Christmas Day and we all went back to the Manor for Christmas Dinner, we could stay with him for the rest of that day, including sleeping there overnight. After having breakfast there on Boxing Day, we could return back here, with your father, in time for lunch, then letting your father stay the night here. He could have breakfast with us before going back to the Manor the next day. In this way, your father would not be left alone over the Christmas period. -Also, the staff would be able to spend a little time together with their families while we are away.'

'That would be an excellent idea,' said Michael. 'Shall we go to the Manor right away and ask my father what he thinks?'

'I will just get my coat on and then we'll go!' Lucy replied.

Mrs Brookes caught sight of Lucy and Michael as they were going towards the study.

'Mrs Brookes! We are just going to see his lordship about Christmas, -that's if he's free?'

'He is,' said Mrs Brookes.

'That's good. I'll come and see you afterwards.'

Michael tapped on the door, 'Can we come in?'

'Yes, come in!' replied his lordship. 'It's nice to see you both!'

'We have something to ask you,' said Michael, '-it concerns Christmas, father. Lucy has had a good idea, so can we let her explain?'

'What is it? Fire away!' said his lordship, with a bemused expression on his face.

When Lucy had finished speaking, Michael's father said, 'I am very touched to think you are bothering about me on this, your first Christmas as man and wife, and I am extremely happy with what you have just suggested, Lucy, especially as the staff at both places will have a chance to be with their families, albeit only for a short time. It's a very nice thought. Would you, Lucy, have a word with Mrs Brookes about it?'

'Yes, I will,' said Lucy. 'She was enquiring about Christmas earlier.'

'I suppose your mother and father will be alone this Christmas, for the first time since they had you?' said Lord Barnes.

'Yes,' replied Lucy. 'It will be strange for them.'

'Would you like to ask them here for Christmas Dinner, and to stay until the evening?'

'That's very kind of you,' replied Lucy, 'I will ask them. There is one other thought, my lord, -could we have a Christmas tree from the Estate at our house please? I was going to mention it to Michael, but with one thing and another, it slipped my mind!'

'Of course you can,' said his lordship.

'I expect you have one here at the Manor?' enquired Lucy.

'Well, no,' replied his lordship, '-but if you think it would be nice, well, let us have one here too! Have a word with Mr Parry, Michael, and tell him what you want. He will soon fix you up!'

Feeling very pleased with the outcome of their meeting, Michael and Lucy went in search of Mrs Brookes. Lucy said to Michael, 'This will take a little while - if you want to, you could go and find Mr Parry about the Christmas trees!'

'Alright,' replied Michael, 'I will see you later, at home.'

When Lucy had finished telling Mrs Brookes all about the Christmas plans, Mrs Brookes was delighted. She said, 'I have always wanted to see a Christmas tree here at the Manor, but with only his lordship here, it didn't seem worth all the fuss on Christmas Day.' Mrs Brookes went on, 'Agnes can replace Freda in the kitchen, so Freda will have the day off, and on Boxing Day, Freda can work down at the Gatehouse with Mrs Judd, and Agnes will have the day off.'

Lucy said, 'That sounds workable. I must tell Mrs Craddock what we have decided.'

When Mrs Brookes told the staff at the Manor about the Christmas arrangements, they were very pleased, '-And to think we will be having a Christmas tree here at the Manor!' said Florence.

'I wonder who will be given the job of decorating it? We always have one at home,' said Maud. 'My mother and I usually put colourful decorations on our tree - it looks so lovely! His lordship lets the staff have holly and mistletoe from the woods, and sometimes we find chestnuts which we roast on the fire hob.'

'I think I heard Mrs Plum say his lordship is having a goose for Christmas dinner,' said Florence, '-and now he is inviting Mr Michael and Miss Lucy, and Miss Lucy's parents here for Christmas Day, he will need a very big one! Then they are going down to the Old Gatehouse on Boxing Day, and we shall have most of the day off. My mum will be pleased when I tell her.'

Meanwhile, back at the Old Gatehouse, a triumphant Mrs Judd proudly presented a Christmas cake which she had just taken out of the oven.

'Well done!' exclaimed Mrs Craddock.

'Yes, very well done!' said Lucy. 'It's a lovely Christmas cake.'

'Shall we try a piece?' said Michael jokingly.

'Not until Christmas time!' said Lucy, with a smile.

There was a general sense of relief as everyone knew there was more at stake than just a Christmas cake! If Mrs Judd had handed her notice in, Lucy would be looking for a new cook, and that would have been problematic just before Christmas.

Later on that day, a worried Nigel Blair went to see Lord Barnes. Mrs Brookes showed him into the study.

'His lordship won't be long, Mr Blair.'

'Thank you, Mrs Brookes.'

After a few minutes, Lord Barnes came in. 'Good afternoon, Nigel.'

'Good afternoon, your lordship. I thought I best come

and see you about the dairy farm. For a while now, people from the village have been coming to the dairy for milk. Ever since Fred Long gave up his milk-round, we have been getting more and more people each week. At present, we have enough cows to supply the milk, but very soon, I doubt we will have enough milk to go round, particularly with Christmas just round the corner.'

'What do you advise, Nigel?' asked his lordship.

'Well,' replied Nigel Blair, 'to start with, we ought to buy two or three more cows and we will need more help in the dairy. My daughter, Phillis, has been helping out on occasion, but she will be away from home after Christmas. Sally and Ivy, who work full-time in the dairy, are finding it difficult to keep up with the increased workload.'

'I can see you have got more on your plate than you should have,' said his lordship. 'Is there anyone on the Estate who could take over as manager of the dairy farm?'

'Yes, your lordship, -George Sharp, who works on the farm already, has often helped me when I have had to deal with a difficult calving. His daughter, Freda, works in the kitchen here at the Manor. He likes working with cattle.'

'It sounds to me as if we have the solution to the problem,' said his lordship. 'Get him to come and see me, and if we offer him the job, perhaps you might keep an eye on him to start with? By the way, Nigel, it was your son who came to the rescue when I fell off my horse, what's he doing now?'

'Well, my lord, he has left school and is looking for work. As a matter of fact, he would be useful helping out in the dairy, lifting the milk churns about. He's a strong boy despite his size.'

'Tell Mr Parry to set him on then, he's a good lad and will be a help, I'm sure,' said his lordship. 'Will you also tell Mr Parry I shall be seeing George Sharp? The sooner we get this started, the better. Take my son, Michael, with you when you go to buy those extra cows, -it's time he learnt what to look out for when buying livestock.'

'Thank you, my lord, I will.'

After Nigel Blair had seen Mr Parry, he drove over to the dairy to see how Sally and Ivy were getting on.

'These milk churns don't get any lighter!' said Sally, as she struggled to get one on to the bench.

'Well now, I have just been to see his lordship about some help in here,' replied Nigel, 'and he suggested my son, Albert, who is looking for work now he's left school, so you won't have to lift those milk churns much longer!'

'Oh! That is good news!' said Sally. 'The sooner, the better!'

'We have made some more butter this morning,' said Ivy. 'There's a couple of pails of whey there for the pigs.'

'Right,' said Nigel Blair, 'I'll send Henry round to collect them.'

Next day, Mr Parry arrived with George Sharp to see his lordship. Lord Barnes outlined the duties of a dairy farm manager.

'I understand you are used to working with cattle, and I know Nigel will always help you if you need assistance with any of the stock. Young Albert Blair will be starting work in the dairy, and you can get him to take some of the heavy lifting away from the two young ladies there. It is our intention to increase the herd of cows in order to keep up with the demand for milk and butter. I suggest you go with Nigel and my son when they go to buy more cows.'

'Right y'be, my lord,' replied George Sharp.

'Mr Parry will have a word with the wages clerk to increase your pay to that of manager. I trust I have chosen right by you, so don't let me down.'

'I will do my best to make a go of it, my lord. I have always liked working with cattle and I'm sure I won't let you down. Thank you once again, my lord.'

CHAPTER 29

The next day, Mr Parry arrived at the Manor with a large Christmas tree.

'Where would you like it put, Mrs Brookes?'

'I think it would be best if it stood inside the main hall, so we can get round it to put the decorations on.'

'Right!' said Mr Parry, bringing in a large barrel and putting it into position. Then he went out to his cart, and with the help of one of the farmworkers, carried the Christmas tree inside, ceremoniously placing it into the barrel, which he then proceeded to fill with soil.

Whilst this was going on, Mrs Brookes and Florence

stood by in case their help was needed.

'Is that alright for you, Mrs Brookes?'

'Yes, thank you, Mr Parry.'

'I will leave you to put the fancy bits on!' replied Mr Parry, with a chuckle. 'Now I have got one to take down to the Old Gatehouse for Mr Michael and Miss Lucy. I must be careful not to go into the kitchen, otherwise I will have Mrs Craddock after me!'

When Mr Parry arrived at the Old Gatehouse, he walked round to the back door of the kitchen. Knocking loudly, he called out, 'Is anyone there?'

Suddenly the door opened.

'Sorry about that!' said Mrs Craddock. 'I was in the wash-house helping Mrs Judd fold up some sheets.'

'Where would you like this Christmas tree, Mrs Craddock?'

'Oh…. I must ask Miss Lucy,' said Mrs Craddock, all in a fluster. 'You can come in, Mr Parry.'

'I.. -er, rather not!' replied Mr Parry. 'My boots……'

'Oh, they are alright!' said Mrs Craddock.

Stepping gingerly inside the kitchen, Mr Parry waited while Mrs Craddock went to find Miss Lucy.

'Good morning, Mr Parry!' said Lucy, as she entered the kitchen. 'Have you brought our Christmas tree?'

'That's right, Miss Lucy!' replied Mr Parry. 'I have. Where would you like me to put it?'

'I think it would be nice in the drawing room,' said Lucy. 'I will show you where I would like it to go.'

So carefully taking his boots off, Mr Parry carried first the barrel, and then the tree into the drawing room, placing them where Lucy wanted.

'Thank you, Mr Parry. It's a lovely tree. Now we can get busy decorating it,' said Lucy.

Giving Mrs Craddock a grin, then turning to Lucy, he said jokingly, 'Miss Lucy, did you say Mrs Craddock was going to dance round the tree on Boxing Day?'

'Get away with you!' said Mrs Craddock. 'You're an old tease!'

'That's as may be, but now I must go. Goodbye ladies!'

'Thank you once again,' said Lucy.

After Mr Parry had gone, Mrs Craddock said, 'Have you got any decorations for the tree yet?'

'No, not yet.' replied Lucy, 'I might start by getting a few from home, and I shall also have to go shopping for some. We have always had a Christmas tree, as far as I can remember. Christmas would not be the same without one.'

Back at the Manor, Nigel Blair was crossing the main hall, having been to see his lordship, when he saw Florence and Maud bringing in a box of decorations for the Christmas tree and a tall pair of steps.

'Mind you make a good job of it!' said Nigel, with a chuckle.

'Would you like to put the fairy on the top?' retorted Florence, cheekily.

'Haha! Don't forget the mistletoe!' laughed Nigel, as he went on his way.

'We won't,' replied Florence, making a face at Maud.

Later on, Lord Barnes came out of the study and into the main hall where Florence and Maud were putting the finishing touches to the Christmas tree.

'That looks very nice!' exclaimed his lordship.

'Thank you, my lord,' replied Florence.

'Have you heard the lunchtime gong yet?' he asked.

'Not yet, my lord,' replied Florence.

Just then, Mrs Brookes appeared.

'Has the lunchtime gong been sounded yet, Mrs Brookes?'

'I am just going to do that!' replied Mrs Brookes.

Lord Barnes turned and made his way to the dining room, followed by Mrs Brookes. Florence and Maud stopped what they were doing and made their way to the kitchen to join Mrs Plum and Freda for their lunch.

While they were eating, Florence turned to Freda and said, 'Why was lunch late today?'

'Oh!' whispered Freda, 'Mrs Plum forgot to put the potatoes on!'

'I wondered why they were not mashed! I don't think his lordship was best pleased with lunch being late - I understand he has a meeting to go to this afternoon,' said Florence, 'and this will cut his afternoon nap short!'

Lucy had been out shopping for little gifts for the tree. As she walked into the hall she met Michael and remarked, 'I think it is cold enough for snow. I'm glad Mrs Craddock has seen to getting the house nice and warm.'

'Well,' said Michael, 'there is plenty of coal and wood in the woodshed. Mr Parry has seen to that.'

The next morning, when Lilly took the tea into Michael and Lucy's bedroom, she told them excitedly that it had been snowing in the night, and there was about two inches of snow on the ground.

'A perfect day to decorate the tree!' smiled Lucy, happily.

Just before lunch, she was putting the final touches to it, when Michael walked into the room.

'You've come just at the right time! Will you put the fairy on the top please? I'm not tall enough,' giggled Lucy.

'Ha! - I think even I will need a pair of steps to reach, -but I know who I would like to put up there!' said Michael, jokingly.

'Now then, that's being unkind!' replied Lucy. 'She hasn't done you any harm!'

'You know I don't really mean it! I'll fetch the steps!'

Putting the steps beside the tree, Michael delicately fastened the fairy on to the top branch.

'There!' said Michael. 'Will that do, my sweet one?'

Coming down the steps, Michael said, 'I do think you have made a splendid job of the Christmas tree, it looks very nice - and you made a lot of the decorations yourself! The candle-holders with the barley-twist candles you bought in town look lovely, but those little parcels look even more interesting, -especially the one with an 'M' on it! I wonder who that's for?'

'You'll just have to wait until Christmas Day to find out, won't you?' teased Lucy.

Taking Lucy in his arms, Michael said, 'Now it's time I gave you a kiss!'

'Michael!' exclaimed Lucy, '-someone might come in!'

'Let them!'

'Oh, Michael, you are naughty!'

CHAPTER 30

The next week was spent with the usual festive hustle and bustle leading up to Christmas Day, and the weather lived up to the forecast of frost and snow, making getting about on foot difficult. Finally the day arrived.

The inhabitants of the Old Gatehouse awoke to a bright, sunny morning, with a carpet of snow over everything outside, even the branches of the trees bowed under the weight of the night's snowfall.

'Happy Christmas, Michael!' said Lucy, getting out of bed to look through the window at the snow.

'Happy Christmas to you!' replied Michael, more asleep than awake. 'Have we had much snow?'

'Yes,' replied Lucy, 'quite a lot!'

Just then there was a knock on the door, 'Come in!' called out Lucy, and Mrs Craddock appeared carrying a tea tray. 'Happy Christmas to you, Mrs Craddock,' said Lucy.

'-And a Happy Christmas to both of you.'

'Where is Agnes?' asked Lucy.

'She's helping Mrs Plum at the Manor today and has gone straight there. Mrs Judd was able to get here safely and is cooking breakfast. I will go and get the breakfast table ready.'

'Thank you, Mrs Craddock.'

When Lucy had finished her tea, she turned to speak to Michael, but seeing him with his eyes shut, set about waking him up and what followed next is best left to the imagination! On hearing the rumpus going on overhead, Mrs Craddock, who was preparing the breakfast table below, was heard to say, 'Oh, these young things!'

After breakfast, Michael and Lucy made their way to the church on the edge of the Estate, where they were to join Lord Barnes in the family pews for the traditional Christmas Day service. As they made their way through the snow, Lucy, who was holding on to Michael's arm, said, 'Michael, what about the garden? We won't be there to keep an eye on things.'

'Don't worry,' he replied, 'the Police Inspector said he would have someone keep watch while we were away.'

'Oh, that's fine then,' replied Lucy.

The morning service over, Lord Barnes, Michael and Lucy, along with Lucy's parents, all made their way back to the Manor where Mrs Brookes greeted them with a warming glass of punch in front of a blazing wood fire in the drawing room.

'Come in!' said Lord Barnes, 'and sit where you like. Mrs Brookes has certainly done us proud with this lovely warm fire. This weather will prevent you from working outside, George.'

'Yes, your lordship, but I have been saving up jobs which can be done in the glasshouses. We have got to pot two hundred geranium cuttings so the plants will be ready in the Spring. I have also collected some hollyhock seeds which I intend to plant in pots, and then next year they can be planted out in the border along the south wall of the Manor. They'll make a nice show the following year. We'll also be sowing seeds for some of next year's vegetables.'

'I can see you won't be looking for something to do!' said Lord Barnes with a smile.

'No, my lord,' replied George. 'There's always something wanting to be done!'

'Now I hope we've finished talking about gardening! Once my dad gets going he never stops!' chuckled Lucy.

'You wait, my girl! Where do you think those vegetables came from - the ones you have been eating this year?'

'I'm only pulling your leg!' replied Lucy, with a smile.

'I am sure we are all very grateful to you for supplying us with produce from these gardens,' said Michael. 'As you can see, we look well on them!'

While this was going on, his lordship was sitting by the fire with an amused expression on his face, as his head gardener and daughter exchanged light-hearted banter.

'There,' said Lord Barnes, 'there's the lunchtime gong, shall we go in?'

When they entered the dining room, the smell of roast goose filled the air.

'My, doesn't that smell good?' remarked Lucy's mother as they took their places. His lordship sat at the head of the table, and in front of him was a large dish, upon which was an equally large goose, surrounded by golden roast potatoes.

Then Mrs Brookes and Agnes came in bearing bowls of vegetables and set them down on the table whilst his lordship was carving the goose. Mrs Brookes and Agnes left the room to return to the kitchen, fetching the gravy and the yorkshire pudding.

'My word!' said Lucy's father, 'I'm glad I haven't got to work this afternoon. I shall have a devil of a job to keep awake!'

'That's alright, George,' smiled his lordship. 'I usually have a nap after lunch!'

'I expect Michael and I will go for a walk,' said Lucy.

'I should like to go too!' replied Lucy's mother.

When they had finished the main course and the dirty plates had been removed, Mrs Brookes entered the room carrying the Christmas pudding enveloped in flames, which she proudly set down in front of his lordship.

'That is a wonderful sight, Mrs Brookes!' exclaimed Lord Barnes.

'Thank you,' said Mrs Brookes. 'I hope you all enjoy it. Agnes will be along shortly with the cream and custard. Would you like me to serve tea in the drawing room when you have finished with the port?'

'Yes please, Mrs Brookes. Thank you very much for everything, -and please convey my appreciation to Mrs Plum and the kitchen staff for a splendid meal,' replied his lordship.

After they had finished their lunch, Lord Barnes led the way into the drawing room where Mrs Brookes was busy setting out the cups and saucers.

'It looks like being a nice afternoon for our walk,' remarked Michael.

'I hope so,' replied Lucy.

'That was a wonderful lunch, your lordship,' said Lucy's mother. 'It's been so nice to have somebody else do the cooking!'

'You're very welcome,' replied Lord Barnes, and turning to Mrs Brookes he added, 'thank you again, Mrs Brookes, for all you have done.'

Eventually, Michael, Lucy and Lucy's mother went out for their walk. Lord Barnes said to Lucy's father,

'This is what I've been waiting for -I think it's time for a nap!'

Both men settled down in front of the fire and it wasn't long before they were fast asleep.

When the walkers returned sometime later, Mrs Brookes met them at the door to say the menfolk were still fast asleep!

'I have cleared away the tea things, and will be preparing the dining room for a light evening meal shortly.'

'Thank you,' said Michael, 'but I don't think I could eat anything else at the moment!'

'Nor could I!' replied Lucy's mother.

'Shall we go and see if they really are still asleep?' said Lucy.

As they made their way into the drawing room, Lord Barnes looked up and said, 'I must have dropped off!'

'It looks like both of you dropped off!' replied Michael, with a chuckle.

'Come on George, wake up!' said Lucy's mother, seeing Lucy's father still asleep with his mouth open.

Coming to, he said, 'My, that was a marvellous lunch your lordship, -I think the fire must have sent me off!'

'You were not alone in that!' remarked Lord Barnes. Turning to Michael he asked, 'Have you all had a good walk?'

'Yes, thank you,' replied Michael. 'We went along by the spinney and up as far as the poplars.'

'You certainly have had a good walk!' replied Lord Barnes.

'It's turning bitterly cold out there now,' said Lucy, 'but we shall soon get warm in here with this lovely fire.'

The rest of the day was spent chatting about old times and playing games.

Later that evening, Mrs Brookes came into the room with another bowl of punch. After handing a glass to everyone, she wished them all a Happy Christmas.

'-And a very Happy Christmas to you too, Mrs Brookes!' replied his lordship. 'I don't know when I have enjoyed a Christmas so much. It's lovely to have one's family and friends around at this time of the year.'

Meanwhile, down in the kitchen, Mrs Plum and the rest of the staff were holding their own Christmas festivities in between seeing to the food for his lordship in the dining room.

'Florence, have you been out carol singing this Christmas?' asked Agnes.

'No,' replied Florence, 'but some of my friends have. I went last year and caught a nasty cold, so I gave it a miss this year.'

'I went one night last week,' said Maud, '-with Sally and Ivy from the dairy. They've got Albert Blair helping them now, you know.'

'I think his lordship had something to do with that,' remarked Florence, 'and I am so pleased we shall all be having a day off tomorrow after breakfast, when his lordship goes down to Michael's for the day and night. Just think, we need not be back until eight o'clock the following morning!'

'Mr Parry will be looking in to check the boiler tomorrow afternoon so the house doesn't get cold for when we're back. He's a good sort,' said Maud. 'I hope his lordship doesn't stay up too late tonight.'

'Why?' asked Florence.

'Because if they're late to bed, they'll be up late in the morning, and half the day will be gone before we get away. I'm anxious to get home to see what's in my stocking!' said Maud.

'Some nuts, an orange, a net with sweets in it and a paper hat!' laughed Florence. '-Well, you won't have to wait much longer!'

CHAPTER 31

Boxing Day began bright and sunny, but cold. The inhabitants of the Manor were slow to wake up, having been late to bed the night before. When Mrs Brookes sounded the breakfast gong it was several minutes before anyone appeared, -Michael being the last to arrive! It was evident one or two were suffering from a thick head following the evening's revelries, and as they all took their places at the breakfast table, Lord Barnes remarked, 'I do declare that gong gets louder every time I hear it!'

'I can still hear it in my head now!' said Michael.

Mrs Brookes came into the room to attend to breakfast.

'Good morning to you all,' she said. 'It's a lovely crisp, sunny morning out there.'

'Good morning, Mrs Brookes,' came the half-hearted response.

'I expect you will all be going for a nice long walk when you have had your breakfast?'

'I am not quite sure, Mrs Brookes, what we shall be doing,' replied his lordship.

'All I feel like doing is going back to bed!' said Michael, clearly suffering more than the others from too much indulgence.

'We will all be going to the Old Gatehouse when we leave here,' replied Lucy.

'Mrs Craddock will be expecting us for lunch,' Michael groaned.

'Michael,' said his lordship, 'we could go for a ride after lunch providing it's not too frosty for the horses.'

'Alright,' agreed Michael, not wishing to disappoint his father.

Breakfast over, they all prepared to wend their way to the Old Gatehouse. Lucy's parents decided to go home first and then follow on for lunch.

'I am quite looking forward to this!' remarked Lord Barnes. 'It's the first time my son and his wife have invited me to stay.'

'I hope Mrs Craddock has got everything ready for us,' said Lucy.

When they arrived, Mrs Craddock, who was over-joyed at having his lordship to stay, greeted them and wished them all the compliments of the season.

'Come into the drawing room, there's a lovely warm fire in there, and I will bring you some refreshment.'

'Thank you,' replied Lucy.

Making their way into the drawing room, Lord Barnes remarked how well the old house looked after being refurbished. 'It has certainly made a nice home for you to live in.'

'We are very grateful to you, your lordship, for it,' replied Lucy. 'Michael and I love living here.'

After lunch, Lord Barnes and Michael set off on their ride as it was such a lovely afternoon.

As they drew near to the dairy farm they saw George Sharp, the new dairy farm manager.

'The compliments of the season, my lord!' said George.

'And to you too!' replied his lordship. 'Have you had a good Christmas?'

'Yes, thank you, your lordship, -quite good. One of the young cows decided to calve on Christmas morning, otherwise all was quiet on the farm.'

'How is young Albert Blair getting on?' asked his lordship.

'Oh, I think he likes working in the dairy with Ivy and Sally! In fact, on Christmas Eve when I was doing my rounds, I heard a few screams coming from the dairy, so

I went to investigate, and found young Albert holding a bunch of mistletoe and trying to kiss one of the girls! I think he was attempting to get his own back on them. Since there are two girls they have the upper hand - if you can see what I mean! Otherwise the three get on well together.'

'What it is to be young!' said his lordship, with a smile.

Turning to Michael, Lord Barnes said, 'That young man will make a good manager one day when he is older, and perhaps take over from his father when Nigel is too old to work, so keep that in mind.'

'I will, father,' replied Michael.

When they returned to the Old Gatehouse, Lucy said to Michael, 'Do you think his lordship would mind if the staff came and joined us for some party games after we have had tea?'

'I should think he would be delighted!' replied Michael. 'Seeing how he reacted this afternoon when George Sharp told him how he caught young Albert with the mistletoe, kissing one of the dairymaids, and he just said, 'what it is to be young!' I think it might amuse him. When I can get him alone, I will ask him!' said Michael.

Just then the phone rang in the study. Michael went to answer it. 'You're wanted on the phone, father!'

His lordship rose from his chair and made his way into the study. After he had finished on the phone, Michael said, 'How would you feel if the staff joined us for a few party games after tea in the drawing room, father?'

'Well,' replied his lordship, 'as it is Christmas and I am in your house, I think it might be a lot of fun, -only I do not want to get kissed by Mrs Craddock under the mistletoe, it would be all over the village tomorrow!'

Michael laughed. 'I will tell Lucy. She will be pleased.'

So Lucy went to find Mrs Craddock to tell her that since it was a special occasion, the staff would be welcome to join the family for some party games in the drawing room after tea. Mrs Craddock thought it would be nice for them all to be together, as it was their first Christmas at the Old Gatehouse.

'I will let the others know.'

Tea-time arrived and Lucy took Lord Barnes into the dining room, followed by Michael and Lucy's parents. Mrs Craddock had laid paper hats at all the place settings. Lucy's father was the first to put his on.

'I must say, George, it suits you!' remarked his lordship with a smile.

'You ought to keep it to wear when you are in the glasshouse!' said Lucy, laughing.

'You can guess what the men would say if I did!' retorted Lucy's father.

Michael was pleased that everyone was enjoying themselves, particularly his father, who he wanted to have a really good time. When tea was over, they all made their way to the drawing room, and once everyone had sat down, Lucy said, 'Michael and I thought it would be nice, with his lordship's consent, to ask all the staff to come in and join us for the evening, and so as soon as they have finished their duties, they will come in.'

After a short while, Mrs Craddock appeared, followed by Mrs Judd, Freda and Lilly.

'Come in and sit down,' said Lucy.

Mrs Judd and Freda had both put clean aprons on, while Lilly wore her best dress. Mrs Craddock was her usual self!

'I understand we are going to play party games,' said his lordship. 'I don't know about you, Mrs Craddock, but I hope it does not entail too much running about!'

'I think we must leave that to the younger ones here!' smiled Mrs Craddock.

'I quite agree!'

'I thought we might start with passing the parcel,' said Lucy, excited to think that everyone was going to get a gift.

'We will want music for that,' remarked Michael.

'I will use the phonograph,' said Lucy.

Getting everyone in a circle, Lucy handed the parcel to Michael to start. When the music stopped, Mrs Judd was holding the parcel. Taking the first layer of paper off, Mrs Judd remarked, 'A nice pair of woollen gloves - just what I wanted!'

When the music began again, Mrs Judd gave the parcel to Lilly and so on until the music stopped. This time it was his lordship's turn. Carefully unwrapping the next layer of paper, he exclaimed, 'Some handkerchiefs!

They will be very useful .' -And so the game went on until everyone had received a gift.

'That was a bit of fun!' laughed Freda, who had finished up with a coloured scarf.

'Let's have a game of forfeits!' somebody called out, '-or Blindman's Buff!'

'I do not mind what we play,' thought Michael, 'as long as I do not have to pay a forfeit with Mrs Judd!'

'Now, I think it's time to see what we've got on the tree,' said Lucy, excitedly.

'It seems a shame to spoil it,' replied Mrs Judd. 'It looks so beautiful.'

'Nevertheless,' said Lucy, 'there is something here for everyone.'

Taking the presents from the tree, she handed them to Michael, carefully holding back her own, and the parcel with the 'M' on it until last!

After everyone had looked at their presents, Lucy said, 'I think it's time for some punch and a nice mince pie!'

Mrs Craddock and Mrs Judd didn't need telling twice, and wasted no time in carrying through a bowl of punch and a plate of hot mince-pies.

'I do not know when I have enjoyed myself so much!' declared his lordship. 'Being with my family has made this the best Christmas I have ever had.'

'I am so glad. You have been so very kind to us, my lord,' replied Lucy. 'Michael and I are thrilled to have you stay, -and you, Mum and Dad.'

The evening progressed with more games, and liquid refreshment was free-flowing. All too soon it was time for the party to come to an end. Mrs Craddock stood up and thanked Michael and Lucy for inviting all the staff to what had been a very happy evening.

Lucy remarked, 'We have enjoyed your company and before you go, shall we all link arms and sing a verse of 'Old Lang Syne' before the party breaks up? We can practise it for the New Year!'

In spite of the late hour, they did this with gusto, dancing around the Christmas tree, and after all the 'Good Nights' had been said, and the lights had been put out, the family made their way upstairs to bed. It wasn't long before they were fast asleep.

The next day was sunny but cold. There had been more snow during the night, and the occupants of the Old Gatehouse were slow to come to life! One by one, they came down for breakfast. Lucy's parents were the first. Mrs Craddock greeted them with a nice cup of tea.

'We have had more snow in the night,' she said.

'It does make getting about difficult,' Lucy's mother remarked. 'It's been lovely being able to stay here with Lucy. George was saying that he'll be working in the glass-houses for the next few days. He still has a few turnips left in the ground, but if we get more snow he won't be able to find them!'

CHAPTER 32

'I hope the men will be out clearing the village paths today,' sighed Mrs Craddock.

'I expect Nigel Blair has already started clearing the roads around the Estate with the snow plough,' said his lordship.

'It's nice to see the snow, but it leaves an awful mess when it thaws.'

Breakfast over, Michael and his lordship made their way to the study, and Lucy and her parents went into the drawing room where there was a fire blazing away in the fireplace.

'I feel like having another nap!' said Lucy's father, yawning.

'Oh no, you don't!' countered Lucy's mother. 'We ought to be on our way, George, there's things to do.'

'What! -and leave this lovely fire?'

'You can stay as long as you like,' said Lucy.

'I know dear, but you know what it's like after being away from home for a few days. The house will be cold and there's the washing to be done. Then there's the thank-you letters to write.'

Reluctantly, they made their way out into the hall, and as they were putting on their coats, his lordship, who had been talking to Michael in the study, came out and said to Lucy, 'Are your parents going now?'

'Yes, your lordship,' replied Lucy.

'Just wait a minute then, George, and I will give you both a lift home. I don't know how deep the snow is, but we'll give it a try, -it's better than walking.'

After his lordship had put his coat on, he joined Lucy's parents in thanking Michael and Lucy for what had been a wonderful time. '-And now we must say goodbye, and leave you two young things to enjoy the rest of Christmas in each other's company.'

During the next few days, there were further accumulations of snow which had to be heaped up on the road sides. The snow ploughs were constantly in use in the hope of keeping the roads open on the Estate. Work on the land had come to a halt before Christmas, so the farm-workers were now having to clear the snow away, as well as looking after the farm animals.

Lord Barnes had asked Mr Parry to come and see him at the Manor. When he arrived, Mrs Brookes showed him into the study.

'I'm a bit concerned, Mr Parry,' said his lordship, 'about the amount of snow we are having. When it starts to thaw there's going to be a lot of water around. How much work was done on the ditches last autumn?'

'Not as much as I wanted,' answered Mr Parry.

'The reason for my concern is because the sixty acre and forty acre fields are both sown with wheat, and are next to each other with a ditch between them. Was this cleaned out last year?'

'Yes,' replied Mr Parry, 'both those fields are low-lying and are always subject to flooding, so I made sure this time that the ditch between was cleaned out.'

'That's good,' replied his lordship. 'My only hope is that when the snow does go, it goes slowly. Thank you, Mr Parry, you have put my mind at rest - we can do no more.'

New Year's Day arrived and the countryside was still covered with snow. It was a full-time job for the farm-workers to keep the roads and paths on the Estate clear for the villagers, who relied on their visits to the Estate's dairy for their milk and eggs. The staff at the dairy were kept very busy.

The next day, Lord Barnes received a letter from Professor Clifton, telling him that the Court of Enquiry had been set up to convene on the tenth of January, and that he, Professor Clifton, had been asked to attend. He also said that when he had all the relevant information he would contact his lordship and acquaint him with it. Lord Barnes got in touch with Michael and told him of the letter.

'The garden is still covered with snow,' Michael told his father, 'but perhaps at this stage, no one will need to inspect the place where the bodies were found.'

'We shall have to wait until we hear from the Professor to know more.'

When Lord Barnes had finished talking to Michael on the phone, he left the study to speak to Mrs Brookes, who was in her room preparing the menu for the coming week. When his lordship found her, he asked her if she would let him have the end of year house accounts.

'Certainly your lordship, I have them here.'

'Thank you, Mrs Brookes,' said his lordship, 'I don't know what I'd do without you. How are the staff managing to get to work in this snow?'

'With some difficulty, my lord,' said Mrs Brookes, with a wry smile.

'Well, if it would help, they could stay here overnight. Perhaps you would have a word with everyone?'

'I will,' replied Mrs Brookes. 'I don't know when we have had as much snow as this before. There will be a lot of water about when the snow melts.'

'That's what I'm afraid of!' replied his lordship. 'We must keep the house warm. There's plenty of wood in the woodshed, thanks to Mr Parry. Well, I must get back to the study with these accounts.'

At the Old Gatehouse, Lucy and Michael were busy taking down the Christmas decorations.

'Doesn't everywhere look bare now that all the cards have gone?' said Lucy.

'I will take the tree into the wash-house for the time being,' replied Michael, 'and then we can plant it in the garden later on. I shall be glad when we know the outcome of the court hearing, then we will be able to get our garden back to normal. Your father wanted to know what we would be doing with the room we found, but I told him we were waiting until we heard from the Professor about the Enquiry.'

'Well,' said Lucy, we haven't got to wait much longer. Your father said he would let us know as soon as the Professor got in touch with him, and that we should know something in ten days' time.'

'I do hope so,' said Michael. 'Oh, I shall be glad when the spring comes - we can try the boat out then. It's in the boathouse at the moment so it's quite safe.'

'Have you given it a name yet?' enquired Lucy.

'No,' replied Michael. 'I thought perhaps you might think of a suitable name.'

'I shall have to put my thinking cap on!' said Lucy.

'Hmmm. -What about Matilda?' enquired Michael.

'Oh no!' said Lucy. 'That's Mrs Judd's name!'

'I'm sure she would feel honoured that we had chosen her name for our boat!' replied Michael, with a laugh.

'The next thing would be that she'd ask you to take her out in it for a sail!' said Lucy, jokingly.

'Heaven forbid!' replied Michael. 'Just think of it!'

'I am!' said Lucy, laughing.

'Then Mrs Craddock would want to come too, -now that would be something!'

'I think we had better change the subject,' said Lucy. 'I must get on sorting these cards out, but before you go, Michael, I have something to ask you, -how many did you say the boat can carry?'

'Why?' asked Michael.

'Well,' said Lucy, 'there may be three of us in the autumn!'

'Lucy, you don't mean…?'

'Yes, I do,' replied Lucy. 'You will be a father in the autumn, Michael!'

'Oh, Lucy, Lucy!' cried Michael, 'I do love you so. Let me take you in my arms, you clever girl. Wait till I tell father - he will be so pleased! Have you told anyone else yet, Lucy?'

'No, I wanted you to be the first to know, Michael.'

'We must tell your parents, Lucy - they will be so excited!'

'I think my mother suspects something, although she didn't say anything to me when they were staying here. Let's call it a woman's intuition!' replied Lucy.

'Well,' said Michael, 'you must take great care of yourself from now on, Lucy, and have all the right sort of things to eat. I expect your mother will be able to advise you on what is good for you. -Oh, I'm overwhelmed with joy!' cried Michael.

Just then, Mrs Craddock came into the room to speak to Lucy, and seeing them both very animated about something, said, 'Is everything alright?'

'Yes, Mrs Craddock,' replied Michael. 'My wife has just told me that I am going to be a father in the autumn!'

'Congratulations!' said Mrs Craddock, 'I am delighted. Have you told your parents yet, Miss Lucy?'

'No,' said Lucy, 'we're going to tell them after lunch, and then we will go on to the Manor to tell Michael's father, so please don't say anything yet!'

CHAPTER 33

When they had finished their lunch, they set off to see Lucy's parents. They found Mrs Fanshaw at home. Lucy said, 'Mother, we have something to tell you. I'm expecting a baby in the autumn and you are going to be a grandmother!'

'Oh, my dear, I am so pleased. Congratulations to both of you!' exclaimed Lucy's mother. 'I must say your father will be delighted, -he was only saying the other evening, 'I wonder when my daughter will make me a grandfather?' '

'Michael and I are going over to the Manor to give

Michael's father the news, so we will call in on Dad at the same time,' said Lucy.

Making their way over to the Manor, they found Lord Barnes talking to Mrs Brookes in the hallway.

'Hello, father!' said Michael, 'we've come to see you to give you some good news!'

'Well, that's what I like to hear, isn't it, Lucy? That will be all for now, Mrs Brookes.'

Once they were on their own, Michael announced, 'We are going to make you a grandfather in the autumn!'

'Bless my soul!' said his lordship, 'that is good news! Congratulations to you both. I am so pleased for you. Your father will be too, Lucy.'

'Yes, your lordship. We are going to find him now to tell him,' said Lucy.

'I should like to see his face when you do!' smiled Lord Barnes. 'You will have to get a nursery ready for my grandchild, Michael!'

'Yes, I know, father, but the baby isn't due until the autumn so there's plenty of time.'

'I know,' said his lordship, '-but these things have to be prepared beforehand.'

'Well,' said Lucy, 'we must go and give my father the good news!'

Michael and Lucy left his lordship in a felicitous state, and made their way through the kitchens to the glasshouse where Lucy's father was working, together with three members of his staff. When Lucy's father saw

Michael and Lucy, his first thought was that something had happened to his wife.

'We have brought you some good news, Dad,' said Lucy, flinging her arms round his neck. 'You are going to be a grandfather in the autumn!'

'Oh my dear girl, that's wonderful news!' said Lucy's father. Congratulations, I am so very happy for you both.'

Shaking Michael by the hand and giving his daughter a big kiss, he said, 'Have you told your mother yet?'

'Yes, Dad, we have.'

'What did she say?'

'She was delighted,' said Lucy.

'Well, I never did!' said Lucy's father. 'Me - a grandfather!'

'Have you told your father, Michael?'

'Yes, we have just been to the Manor,' said Michael.

'Whatever did he say?'

'Like you, he was very pleased, though I think it rather took him by surprise. I should think he is still sitting in the study in shock!'

'Well,' said Lucy, 'our child will have the best two grandfathers anyone could want. Now we must go home, Michael, there are things to be done!'

Mrs Brookes went into the kitchen to see Mrs Plum about the evening's menu.

'I think his lordship has just been given some good news,' remarked Mrs Brookes. 'Michael and Lucy have been to see him in the study and there was such excitement!'

'They came through here to go and see Lucy's father,' said Mrs Plum. 'I wonder if Lucy's expecting?'

'That could be,' said Mrs Brookes.

It was then that his lordship came into the kitchen.

'I thought you would like to know my son and his wife are making me a grandfather in the autumn - they have just been to tell me.'

'Congratulations, my lord,' said Mrs Brookes.

'That is good news!' said Mrs Plum. 'Now Lucy must take care of herself until the child is born.'

'I'm sure she will,' replied his lordship.

'They will have to start thinking about names to call the baby,' said Mrs Brookes.

'Yes,' agreed his lordship, 'we shall have to wait and see what Michael and Lucy decide.'

When his lordship had left the kitchen, Freda said, 'I have never seen his lordship so happy about anything before!'

'He is clearly delighted at the thought of becoming a grandfather,' replied Mrs Brookes.

'Well, I hope everything goes alright for them,' said Mrs Plum. 'Michael and Lucy are a lovely couple. I'm sure his lordship will see everything is alright for them.'

As the days went by, the news soon spread that Lucy was expecting a baby.

'I wonder where the baby will be born? Here, or down at the Old Gatehouse?' said Florence.

'I should think his lordship would rather Miss Lucy came here,' remarked Maud.

'Well, the weather will be better in the autumn,' added Florence, 'all this snow is getting me down. Day after day and still no let-up! It's like walking in a ghost town when you go outside, everywhere is so quiet and all you can see is snow!'

'Never mind,' said Maud. 'It won't last forever.'

'I suppose when it does go we shall have water every-where!' exclaimed Florence.

'You are cheerful today,' said Maud, laughing. 'Come on, let's get these beds made.'

'You can understand people would rather be in their own houses in this weather instead of going visiting folk,' reflected Florence.

'Yes, I would much rather be in front of a nice fire in this sort of weather,' said Maud.

'So would I,' said Florence. 'By the way, Maud, how did Freda get on helping Mrs Judd down at the Old Gatehouse over Christmas?'

'She said they had a jolly good time. All the staff were invited to play games with the family during the evening.'

'What? - with his lordship?'

'Yes,' said Maud. 'He really did enjoy himself! I think it was great fun by what Freda said!'

'Wonders will never cease!' remarked Florence. 'I

wonder if his lordship was caught under the mistletoe by Mrs Judd?'

'She wouldn't dare, - would she?' asked Maud, giggling.

'That woman is capable of anything when it suits her, -especially if she has had one or two drinks inside her!' declared Florence, with a laugh.

CHAPTER 34

Early in the New Year, a decision was made to bury the remains of the two bodies found at the Old Gatehouse, in the local churchyard. Since there was no further information as to who they were, there would be just a very short service before the remains were interred. This was attended by Lord Barnes, Michael and Lucy, along with the Police Inspector and representatives from the local authority. The Enquiry to determine ownership of the coins was to be held two days later and the police Inspector said he would report back on the Court's findings.

'I shall be glad when this is all over,' said Michael.

'So shall I,' replied Lord Barnes. 'I am relieved that we haven't had any more snow - in fact, it looks as if it's slowly thawing. As you know, I have been concerned about the two fields of winter wheat. They both lie on low ground, but we usually get good results from there.'

'I shall be seeing Nigel this afternoon,' said Michael, 'so I will ask him how things are.'

'Good,' replied Lord Barnes.

When Michael arrived at the farm, he found Nigel Blair sorting out a pile of sacks in the barn. After enquiring about the two fields in question, Michael said, 'How is young Albert getting on at the dairy?'

'Oh,' replied Nigel, with a smile, 'I think he is enjoying himself!'

'How is he getting on with the two girls?'

'I don't think he has developed any amorous feelings for them yet!' said Nigel, with a chuckle. 'There are two of them, so I think they keep him in order! He's a great help in lifting the milk churns around the dairy.'

'That's good,' replied Michael.

At last, the day of the Enquiry arrived. Lord Barnes was in his study when the phone rang. It was the Professor, who said he would like to visit his lordship in two days' time to impart the results of the Court of Enquiry. Lord Barnes thought he ought to let Michael know, so they could both be available when the Professor visited.

Just then, there came a knock on the study door.

'Come in,' said his lordship. The door opened and a harassed Mrs Brookes came in.

'Is everything alright, Mrs Brookes?' asked his lordship.

'I'm having trouble with reporters at the front door, my lord.'

'They're not inside are they?'

'No, my lord, but I would not put it past them to try to force their way in. They seem determined to see you.'

'We will soon see about that!' said his lordship, picking up the phone to the local police station.

'This is Lord Barnes from the Manor, -I'm having trouble with reporters at my front door. Would you please remove them for me?' said Lord Barnes. Then replacing the phone he said, 'I expect it is in connection with today's Enquiry, Mrs Brookes.'

'Thank you, my lord. I can go now and get on with my work without worry.'

'Before you go, will you tell the staff not to say anything to the reporters if asked?'

'I will, my lord.'

'I must warn Michael and Lucy. I hope they don't go bothering them.'

Michael was in his study when the phone rang.

'Good morning, Michael!'

'Good morning, father!'

'I'm having trouble with reporters at my door, so I

have contacted the local police. Be on your guard in case they come bothering you.'

'Oh, you need not worry, Mrs Judd will soon see them off!' said Michael, jokingly. 'She is better than an alsatian dog when she wants to be! -A formidable woman!'

'Well, you know her better than I do!' chuckled Lord Barnes.

After speaking to his father, Michael went to tell Lucy what had been said.

'I will tell Mrs Craddock to be on her guard,' said Lucy. The rest of the day passed without trouble.

On the day of the Professor's visit, Michael and Lucy went up to the Manor to wait with his lordship for the Professor to arrive. When he did, Mrs Brookes answered the door. 'I expect you've come to see his lordship!'

'That's right,' replied the Professor.

'Follow me,' said Mrs Brookes, 'and I will take you to him.' Tapping on the study door, she showed the Professor in.

'Good morning, Professor. Have you had a good journey?' enquired Lord Barnes.

'Yes, thank you,' replied the Professor. 'Now, to get down to business: the Enquiry only lasted two and a half hours. It was thought that the two bodies found in your tunnel room belonged to cavaliers who had been on their way to secure a passage for none other than King Charles himself! It seems likely they were pursued by some of Cromwell's men, and so took refuge in the building now known as the Old Gatehouse, with it's secret tunnel leading down to the chamber where you found them. Unfortunately, with Cromwell's men occupying the surrounding area, escape was impossible. We think the two men would have been shut up in that room with no chance of escape and no food or water. It must have been a terrible way to die.'

He continued, 'Now, concerning the two pouches containing the coins. After some deliberation, the Enquiry decided they should remain the property of the Crown, but that a reward be offered to you, as the owner of the property where they were discovered. You are at liberty to do whatever you like with the tunnel and the chamber, -whether you keep them private, or show them off to the public. As I said, it is believed that the money carried by the two men was to secure a passage for the King to France, -although we now know that he escaped by another route.'

'Well, I never!' said Lucy. 'To think those two men lay dead at the bottom of our garden all those years!'

'It is thought there might once have been an escape door out of the chamber into the building above, which had the mosaic as it's floor, and then away to the lake. The mosaic floor provides evidence of a building having been there before. The Police Inspector will be calling on you regarding the reward, my lord,' said the Professor. 'There were twenty-five gold coins in each pouch. Now, as far as the swords are concerned, no decision has yet been made.

If I hear anything further, I will let you know.'

'Thank you, Professor,' said Lord Barnes. 'You have given us a thorough account of everything and I can't thank you enough. Now, will you stay for lunch?'

'Yes. please,' replied the Professor, 'but I would like to catch the three o'clock train back if I can. Have you thought at all what you might do with the chamber and the tunnel?'

'No,' said Lord Barnes. 'Not yet, but I rather think it is up to Michael and Lucy as it's their garden.'

'Lucy and I have been thinking,' replied Michael, 'that it would be best if the tunnel and chamber be left as they are, out of respect for the two men who died there, but to be sealed off for safety. Then the garden can be returned to it's normal state. We don't want to capitalize on the misfortune of others.'

'Thinking about it,' said Lord Barnes, 'that would be the best solution.'

After the Professor had left, Lord Barnes said he would ask Mr Parry to reinstate the garden by sealing off the chamber and the tunnel so no accidents could occur. Michael and Lucy both agreed that it should be done as soon as possible.

Lord Barnes lost no time in contacting Mr Parry. After he had detailed what was to be done, his lordship enquired how things were on the farm.

'As far as the workforce is concerned,' said Mr Parry, 'when they have finished looking after the livestock, their time is spent cutting up logs, which are then sold in the village. There were several trees blown down during the last gale, and we have been able to sell several loads of logs during this cold spell which is helping to offset wages. Then there is a certain amount of repair work and maintenance being carried out on some of the farm machinery.'

'That's good,' said his lordship, 'thank you, Mr Parry. I'll let you get on with your work!'

'Good day, my lord,' said Mr Parry.

After he had gone, Lord Barnes asked Mrs Brookes to come and see him.

'Mrs Brookes, I have to go up to town tomorrow morning to attend a ceremonial function, would you please see that my clothes are in order for that occasion?'

'I will, my lord,' replied Mrs Brookes. 'Shall I make sure the carriage is ready to take you to the station?'

'Yes, please,' replied his lordship. 'I must just let Michael know that I shall be away for a day or two.'

When the phone rang in the office of the Old Gatehouse, Lucy answered it.

'Is Michael there?' enquired Lord Barnes, once he had asked how she was feeling.

'Yes, indeed, I will fetch him. He is trying to sort out a problem in the wash-house.'

When Lucy entered the wash-house, she found it full of steam. Mrs Judd was all hot and bothered as she stood by the sink in front of a scrubbing board, wielding a large bar of Sunlight soap, which she was applying vigorously to the mud at the bottom of a pair of Michael's old trousers.

Seeing Michael, Lucy said, 'You are wanted on the phone.'

'Who is it?' enquired Michael.

'It's your father, Michael.'

When Michael had gone, Lucy turned to see how Mrs Judd was getting on.

'I shouldn't worry too much about those, Mrs Judd. They're only an old pair of trousers Michael puts on when he goes to the farm to help Nigel Blair with the animals.'

'It's alright, Miss Lucy, I think I have got them clean now!'

'You're a marvel, Mrs Judd!'

CHAPTER 35

During the next few weeks, the weather was in keeping with that typical of mid-February. The slow thaw continued, and all eyes were on the dykes to make sure they would be able to carry the expected amount of water as the snow melted. As the days went by, a spell of wet weather set in, and gradually the snow disappeared. Lord Barnes instructed Mr Parry to visit the two wheat fields twice a day. The month of March came in like a lion, with trees being blown down and gusts of wind almost wrenching the clothes off the washing-line. It did have one advantage, in that the ground was starting to dry out, and as far as the land was concerned, there were no reports of flooding. In Michael's garden, Mr Parry had back-filled the hole over the tunnel, and Lucy's father was busy getting things ready for planting. As the tunnel was not going to be used, Michael and Lucy decided to put a set of cupboards on top of the trap door in the lobby, making more storage in the house.

Now that the days were pulling out, Michael thought he would start getting the boat ready for when the warm weather came, enlisting the help of Nigel Blair. The lake at the Manor was in the shape of a horseshoe, with a small island covered with trees and bushes, and somewhere to moor a boat. Michael had been told by his father that it was a nice place to have a picnic and thought he would like to take Lucy there when the weather improved.

As the days got longer and warmer, Michael took his boat out on the lake. Sailing past the island, he saw the place where he could land - just as his father had mentioned. When he returned to the house, he told Lucy all about it. 'Would you like to see the island, Lucy?'

'Yes, I would,' she replied.

'Very well,' said Michael, 'let's go tomorrow afternoon if the weather is nice.'

'I will ask Mrs Judd to make up a picnic basket for us,' said Lucy.

'That will be lovely,' smiled Michael.

'By the way, your father phoned while you were out on the lake. He wanted you to contact him when you came in.'

'I will phone him now.'

When Michael returned to the drawing room, he told Lucy that his father had got some very good news to impart, and requested they see him as soon as possible.

'Whatever can it be? We'd better go now,' said Lucy.

Making their way to the Manor, they saw a police car standing outside.

'I hope all is well,' said Michael, as they drew near.

Mrs Brookes opened the door and exclaimed, 'Oh, I'm so glad you have come, I will take you to see his lordship!'

When Michael opened the study door, he saw a gaunt-looking figure standing beside his father. Recognising him immediately, Michael cried out, 'William!' as he rushed forward, flinging his arms around his brother, tears streaming down his face. 'You're alive! Where have you been? Are you alright?'

'Steady on,' said Lord Barnes, visibly moved, also with tears in his eyes. 'William has been in the wars quite badly. We have got to thank the Inspector for finding him and getting him back to us when we had all given up hope that he was still alive. It hasn't been an easy task.'

Michael said, 'William, this is my wife, Lucy. We're expecting our first child in the autumn. -Well, I can't get over it! I have a brother now, besides a lovely wife and a very kind father, what more can a man want?'

He sat down, his eyes transfixed on his brother, as if it was all a dream.

'Your brother has had a rough time, Michael, so he will want very careful handling,' said the Inspector.

'We will do all we can to help him recover,' replied his lordship.

'I'm sure you will,' said the Inspector.

'Michael, why don't you and Lucy take William into the drawing room and I will join you as soon as I have had a further word with the Inspector.'

'Very well, father,' replied Michael, putting his arm around his brother and guiding him out of the study. 'Oh, William, I never thought I would see you again, whatever happened?'

'It's quite a story. How have you finished up here?'

'All in good time. We have so much to talk about, but first we must make you comfortable and get you well. I hope you will make your home here at the Manor now.'

'I think I've been given your old room, Michael,' said William.

'That's a very nice room,' replied Lucy, 'with lovely views over the back garden.'

'You know mother died some time ago, William.'

'Yes, father told me.'

'-And Aunt Carry too,' said Michael, as they settled down in the drawing room, 'but first, tell us what happened to you.'

'Well,' said William, 'the last thing I can remember, was when we were on holiday with mother and we both went swimming in the sea. I must have gone out too far, because I was suddenly swept away by the current which kept pulling me away from shore. I tried to call out, but I must have lost consciousness, because when I came to, I found myself lying amongst a lot of sacks in the hold of a ship. A Chinese-looking man gave me a bowl of something to drink, which, as far as I can remember, was not very nice! How long I was there, I do not know. They brought me food and drink and I knew they were trying to help me. After some long time, I was allowed on deck. I remember it was hot when we eventually docked to take on more cargo. After a few more days at sea, we were boarded by officials who took control of the ship, and when the ship docked, we were all put in prison. I tried to protest my innocence, but because of the language barrier, I had trouble making myself understood. How long I was there, I don't know - it must have been years - I was only a boy when it happened! Then one day, quite recently, a detective -who spoke English, came to see me. He had been sent from England to find me, and after asking several questions, said he would bring me back to this country. When I arrived, I was put in a police van and brought here.'

'Well, I think the police have done a wonderful job in finding you and returning you to us. I must thank the Inspector for taking the initiative in following up the account I gave him of your disappearance. He was here on a completely different matter and, now I recall, seemed very interested when I mentioned that your body had never been found.'

'Now, we must get you well, William,' said Lucy. 'His lordship will look after you. Just take things steady and you will soon regain your strength. You and Michael will have lots to talk about! It's lovely to have you back with us.'

'Thank you, Lucy,' replied William.

Just then, Lord Barnes came into the room.

'This is an occasion to celebrate,' he said. 'Now I have two sons to help me run the Estate. I'm overjoyed! Lucy, will you ask Mrs Brookes to bring some wine and to join us for a moment - this is a great day for us as a family.'

'Come in, Mrs Brookes, and join us in celebrating the return of my son, William, who we all thought was dead, but who is alive as you can see, and is here with us today, -thanks to the efforts of the Inspector and his men.'

'That's wonderful news, my lord,' beamed Mrs Brookes.

William's story was reported in the local press. He received several letters of congratulations, and one of these was from Robert, his cousin, who said he would very much like to come to see him. During the next few days, William was kept busy answering them.

Lucy soon found that Michael was spending more and more time up at the Manor with William. She understood this, but there were times when she wished he was with her, especially as it was now very evident that she was expecting her first child. Lord Barnes had suggested Michael and Lucy live at the Manor just prior to the baby being born, as there was room for the nurse and midwife to be accommodated there too, and they would be on hand when the time came. His lordship was not going to have anything go wrong with his first grandchild if he could prevent it.

At the Old Gatehouse, Michael and Lucy had been preparing the new spare bedroom as a nursery. This was next door to Lilly's room. Once the baby was born, Lilly would move into one of the other rooms, making way for a nurse to be on hand to help Lucy with the new arrival. Michael thought this would enable Lucy to recover after the birth, and give his child a good start in life. Everything that could be done, would be done in readiness for the baby.

'Well,' said Michael, as he sat down beside Lucy. 'What a lot has happened since we met. I have a lovely wife who is going to make me a father in the autumn, and my brother is alive and back with his family. I know all of this is giving my father a new lease of life.'

'Yes, William coming back means your father has company up at the Manor. I noticed how much he missed having you around when we moved in here,' remarked Lucy. 'Shall we ask them if they would both like to come for Sunday lunch? I could see whether Mum and Dad are free as well. What do you think?'

'I think that's a very good idea. Let's go and ask them!'

So, the following Sunday, they were all seated around the table at the Old Gatehouse, having enjoyed one of Mrs Judd's 'Sunday Specials', when Lord Barnes rose to his feet, glass in hand, and said, 'Thank you, Michael and Lucy, that was a jolly fine lunch! -and while I'm about it, I would just like to say how very much it means to me to be here today with you all.'

Looking round the table at the warm and friendly faces, he continued, 'Since returning from my travels, fate has been good to me. I now have a real family again, something I least expected, and it's made me a very happy man, so please join me in raising your glasses… I give you a toast: 'Our family!' '

THE END

About the Author

Stanley Scott was born in Ely, and grew up in the West Fen where his father had a dairy farm.

His maternal grandmother had been lady-in-waiting to Lady Leicester at Holkham Hall, and lived with Stanley, his parents and four siblings when he was a boy. He was a chorister at Ely Cathedral, following in his brothers' footsteps, and rose to the heights of Head Chorister, singing on until his voice broke at the age of fifteen and a half.

Being interested in both electricity and water, he started work in the electrical industry at a time when supply companies were eager to promote their product. He later put these skills to good use on becoming involved in the construction and day-to-day running of Grafham Water, where he remained until he retired.

Since then, he has had several other interests, including making houses and shops for his oo gauge model railway town, illuminating the buildings and making the trains do things they were probably never expected to!

At the age of ninety three, he invested in a chrome book and began writing 'The Old Gatehouse', in which some of the story lines are based on real-life happenings, though with a totally fictitious cast.

He is currently engaged on a sequel to 'The Old Gatehouse', and is author of 'The Adventures of Hayley'- six stories for children.

Lightning Source UK Ltd.
Milton Keynes UK
UKHW022248311021
393171UK00009B/225